LAWRENCE FERLINGHETTI

HER

A NEW DIRECTIONS PAPERBOOK

To K

Those who have not insisted, at least once, on the absolute virginity of human beings and of the world, who have not trembled with longing and impotence at the fact that it is impossible, and have then not been destroyed by trying to love halfheartedly, perpetually forced back upon their longing for the absolute, cannot understand the realities of rebellion and its ravening desire for destruction.

Albert Camus

I

I was bearing a white phallus through the wood of the world, I was looking for a place to plunge it, a place to surrender it. Someone had been dragging the earth with a very small plow, about the size of a pocketcomb, a tiny celluloid pocketcomb, such as children find in crackerjack boxes. Or one of those horserakes farmers draw across fields, combing the long hair. It was a transaction with myself, and the scene corresponded almost exactly to reality, the negative of it having slipped just a very little while being printed. Like an extra in a grade B movie, I could not walk out of it, trapped in

9

the celluloid sequence. Or like the grade B hero himself, his images dark, coiled, waiting, creeping round and forward on the unwinding reel, toward that point at which with a whir he would spring upon the screen in a single continuous moment of illumination. In an instant he'd fall into dark again, recoiled, withdrawn within himself, his ten million images coiled again in the can, only one of them ever illuminated at once. It was the dark of the world in which I lay, dreaming of breasts and vulvas. It was a battle with the image, and existence a coiling and recoiling of one's self, with the plot spinning out so smoothly always, although one never could be certain just where one had come in. Added to this was the fact that someone seemed always to be rewinding and restarting the story, each time at a different point. And the first figure one saw not necessarily the main character.

I was looking for the main character of my life, blundering along, stopping for an absinthe here, a coffee there, following the daylight ghosts of myself through the continuous landscape, death and resurrection in a tongue alack. Perhaps I was merely a dumb member of the audience strayed onto the stage by mistake, looking for some printed program he had dropped under a seat. I had somewhere dropped the key that explained the action, and one could not tell the players without a program, for the faces interchanged, fused together. There they moved on their dark illuminated field, playing their curious night-game, bounding after stray balls, winding their pitches on

10

grassless mounds, or squatting behind a batter in their tools of ignorance. I was a world's catcher, I crouched there, wearing my tools, a fat receiver. I received signals, sent out signals to others, squatting with signal fingers hanging down between my legs, crooking a penis finger now and then, calling someone in. They all moved too far out, other figures ran, white celluloid shadows, as in a strip of film held up to light, and the film running away with them. I could not catch them, and they ran off through the streets of the world, until only one figure was left, a white clay figure I had started with, who might have been myself. It was not. It was a her.

It seemed I would not or could not catch up with her. As she walked, her shadow caught on a tree, fell to the ground and stretched, as if made of rubber bands, no china doll about to break, capable of stretching into any form I imagined, a cicada cry in her mouth. When she stopped and turned at a corner, looking about her, before disappearing in a doorway, a small eternity passed, flickered in the late light. At this moment always a strange thing happened. Her image transformed itself into the picture of a little girl with a hoop in a dirndl dress in an album landscape, as in some old painting seen in a museum long ago. The image recurred, the scene repeated itself on other corners as I walked, the figure of the woman just turning the corner or pausing for a moment while the late traffic passed. Then the image again, of the still girl with the hoop. And it would fade, and I would be following

11

another figure. I was too fat to catch up. I had B.O., I sweated too much, my body always growing, stretching down the street. When I was not looking, the distant figure would not advance. The sequence arrested, she stopped dead when I was not looking, yet started off again simultaneously when my eye fell back on her. Over and over.

Meanwhile the papers were reporting sadists shooting tacks, with rubber bands, at apes in zoos. Or reporting Piblokto madness. Piblokto, first discovered among the Eskimos, now spread over the world, a madness of the long, dark winters. Or, rather, I read about it in the papers that blew in the street, and spread it in imagination around the earth. Men and women seized with uncontrollable frenzies, during which they did all sorts of weird and violent things but rarely hurt themselves or others. They had a complete loss of memory as soon as the attack was over. Piblokto usually occurred in the dead of winter, related to the Eskimos' dread of the long seasonal night The symptoms included: tearing off clothing, their own or others', fleeing, nude or otherwise, across ice and snow, and wandering into mountains. If indoors, the victims ran back and forth in a state of great agitation. If aboard ship, victims purposely paced the decks or climbed the rigging. Or they rolled in snow, jumping into icy water, throwing themselves into snowdrifts. Or raved, shouted, threw around everything in sight, picking up loose objects and tossing them in the air, and kicking at everything, particularly dogs. (Dogs suffered from a form of

12

Piblokto too.) Or the victims picked up and cherished odd things, or gave exhibitions of extreme strength not normally possible. Or went into acts which had the appearance of the beginnings of real violence which, however, never were carried through. Victims were completely exhausted after an attack and slept for as long as two days. Rational behavior immediately followed. Men and women were equally susceptible, but it was a quite different phenomenon from 'running amok,' the tendency of Piblokto victims being to run away from each other, as well as from all others, rather than toward them. The Eskimos considered the attacks as entirely normal and expected them to happen to anybody. They were all running away from me, in the streets, through which I was always walking. Perhaps I myself had Piblokto. One of the latest victims. I had not expected it to happen to me. It was not happening. At any rate, men and women were equally susceptible, running away from each other. Only I was running toward them, as the scene kept recapitulating itself. The night street. The women hurrying away, disappearing. Then the girl with the hoop, motionless, out of a somewhere past. And though often repeated, as if each time I re-entered the movie at the same still point in the film, the sequence was never reversed. That is, the girl with the hoop never appeared first, to be followed by the grown, disappearing woman, which would have seemed to be the logical chronology. Everything else appeared to happen in perfect chronological order, despite the recurrent, almost identical scenes. Only the

13

little girl was out of place. She was certainly out of place in that city, for I saw her always in a lost or dreamed landscape, green and distant. She was certainly out of place on that island in the city, this island that floated in its river through the city and upon which I was always walking, or in that Square to which I returned and returned.

At the end of a series of great wandering circles, I ended there, as if it were there that the real play was to take place, as if it were there that the main action was about to happen or be filmed. I could not tell whether or not I was the grade B hero or merely an extra, any more than I could tell whether or not the action had already been filmed. I seemed to be walking in on the finished sequence only to find myself in the middle of it as it evolved for the first time. I say 'for the first time' as if the scene did not recapitulate itself each time I came. Over and over, always the same. The same café terrace, just off the Square, the same dim lights inside, the same figures on the terrace, the same dim lights inside, the same figures on the terrace, peering out of the little side street into the Square. It was a scene I had already painted in all its parts, a book of photographs I had already thumbed through and digested page by page. I had already painted everybody else's painting of the same subject, and I had torn out all the photos in the picture book and scattered them about on the stones of the Square where they lay still looking up at me like so many disheveled characters, and the figures on the terrace were the propped-up

14

portraits of the same subjects painted and repainted by different hands before me, only the paint had now grown wet again and dripped down, the faces falling apart as in a melting mirror, until all that remained were the bare bones of the leaded canvas and the bare bones of the buildings, all in need of repainting. It had all already happened, as in scenes from a distant life long forgotten and now recollected only in their bare essentials. The figures on the terrace had already happened, and one of them was myself, and one of the other figures had my arm and was shaking it, again. I was the fat one, and I had not known fat had undone so many. The hour was late, and I had my coat collar turned up, as if it were cold on the terrace. Or as if I had been traveling. The old coat collar turned up made me believe I had been traveling. Or perhaps it had been raining and I'd been walking in the rain. There was a small puddle at the edge of the terrace, at the very edge, in which I saw the scene recapitulated upsidedown. I had only to look down into the puddle to see the whole scene arrested in its essence. In black and white, strangely still, the mouth of the older of the two sitting figures caught open, like a mouth on a megaphone mask. The sound that went with the scene was also arrested, and the whole of it—dark buildings, cobbles, church towers, leaves and trees in the Square—suspended in silence. Or in a waiting hush. Everything was waiting. Even the tongue in the open mouth hung suspended, waiting to speak again. Somewhere a toilet flushed. Or a bidet. Then the tongue moved, continued, the leaves stirred

15

again, and whispered about falling. They did not fall, for it was the wrong season, a long spring. That tongue dwelt with a curious, scalding intensity upon what it was saying, as if the words issued from the mouth against its will, as if the tongue tore the words from it and spit them out through the mask of the face, the face itself half-believing what it heard. The face was two masks, a mask of comedy superimposed on one of tragedy, the downturned corners of the hidden mouth showing through the smile of the other. The hand shook my arm, the pigeons whirred in the Square, the church towers leaned over to overhear what was said, then tilted back as I looked up, withdrawing like someone caught listening. Pigeons settled and walked around silent on sea-legs, the Square the edge of some sea-coast and they those gulls that embody drowned sailors' souls.

In the little side street just off the square, at the edge of the café terrace, was the entrance to a small hotel, its door a dark mouth through which a woman's figure might have just passed. I had followed into the Square, from another direction. My feet, tangled in shadow, had lost the track, and wandered about under the trees. I looked down at my feet and saw them, a pair of lost shoes, as enormously weighted as the lead feet one wears in dreams. In dreams of flight or pursuit, the feet, encumbered with huge lead soles, sink through heavy water, while the body still strains forward. My feet were a pair of shoes wandering about the Square, and behind them they furrowed a path, as if with a

16

small plow. Small messenger's wings on the side of each shoe had wilted and drooped down, dragging me to a stop. The little wings were long shoelaces trailing the pavement, and now they had grown down through the pavement, grasping the earth beneath. Like roots. I was growing there, one of the motionless dark trees of the Square, a tree with a fat, clumsy trunk, curiously associated with the still figure of a little girl with a hoop in a dirndl skirt in a lost green landscape. Now that the figure of the grown woman had disappeared around the corner into that little side street, the image of the little girl came back. Only now something was added to the sequence. The figure moved this time, articulated as if by unseen little strings, the way marionettes are moved, from above. The figure of the little girl bent over slowly and reached for a piece of white string that lay innocently enough on the ground. Her small white hand reached out for the little straight string which was as purely white as innocence itself. With the string in its fingers, the little figure straightened up and at once resumed its former fixed pose. But the string had slipped from its fingers. It lay on the ground again innocently enough. The little girl bent over again to retrieve it. Her small white hand, upon which now gleamed a tiny paste gem, reached out slowly, retracted itself for an instant, and reached out slowly again for the pure white string. It was no longer pure white. A tiny streak of mud ran along one side of it where it lay innocently enough. With the string in its fingers again, the little figure straightened up again and at once resumed its former

17

pose, as if waiting for its picture to be taken, or for its portrait to be painted. Only now the tiny streak of mud had transferred itself to her cheek. And the string had fallen again, and the girl bent over again to retrieve it, reached out slowly for it, straightened up again with the string, and at once resumed her former pose, waiting for herself to be taken, a woman waiting to be taken, a tiny streak of lipstick on her cheek. The towers tilted back, and the earth moved, tilting me forward. I could still see the café terrace where the two figures sat, one of them grasping the arm of the other. The other, the fat one, had his collar turned up, as if against the night. In the interior of the building somewhere a toilet flushed. The first figure continued speaking. He was a spielman, a flyman, a world's navel, with a hand that held me. It slipped, raised itself in the air, holding up two spread fingers to a waiter inside the café. The waiter came with his little towel over his arm and a little tray upon which were two green drinks. Some-where down the side street someone had put a record on. The music oozed up the street, and it wasn't a rec-ord, it was an accordion man on a far corner by a Metro entrance, squeezing his pleated sad box. The one that had gripped my arm now swayed on his seat to the music, mimicking the accordionist with his arms, flap-ping them like some great bird of prey come to roost. He crooned a burlesque imitation. His voice cracked, and he coughed. The music continued to go round, the night went round with it. '*Garçon.*' The two spread fin-gers waved, the waiter came again with his towel on his

18

arm and a little tray upon which rested two green drinks. The music had faded, all faded with it, and the wicker chairs put up on the tables, upsidedown, the puddle at the very edge of the terrace reflected right-side-up, rehearsing the scene in reverse, though the chairs were now empty, the café itself now shuttered, the hotel's door at the side of the terrace in deeper shadow, under a dim smoked bulb. I was moving away from that mouth with its cigarette butt of a bulb still smoking in it.

I was going toward the river with my leaded feet. They struck hollow on the cobbles of the descending street, as if I were already underwater. I fell through the aqueous air like a sinking swimmer, past two sunk churches and on toward the Seine and its two anchored islands. I saw my body growing in the waters of it, like one of those islands, half-submerged. I had died and I could prove it; it was in the papers, in the morning papers. I had skimmed a dime over a fair and won a cockatoo and had then stolen some white string to use as a leash for the bird, and they had caught me at it and exiled me to spend the rest of my life picking up string in the streets of Paris. I used to steal things when I was a kid, and they'd now found me out, but I'd just escaped to my own death. I used to collect string when I was a kid, then had branched out into tinfoil, which I rolled into great balls. Then I'd started on keys and rings, hoarding them like a magpie, making regular little nests of them in the attic. Then knives and forks from dining halls or restaurants. Until they found me

19

once with a whole cache of them in a closet. Now they'd come after me again, long afterward, still looking for my childhood thefts, but I'd outfoxed them all now, by furnishing them with a fresh death. There was some kind of paper stuck to one of my shoes, streaked with dirt. I reached down and picked it up. There was my picture to prove my death, with a caption under it, explaining it all, and I saw now that no one had been after me for long-ago conneries, I had imagined it all. A tiny streak of mud ran along one side of the paper, and under the picture the black printing began, set in immovable type. The paper slipped from my hand, I bent to retrieve it. New streaks of mud now covered parts of the text: *at Notre Dame during Lent*   *after having fallen from one of the towers which he had climbed by means of a scaffold set up around it for repairs*
not clear as to whether   *fell by accident or jumped to*   *Certain singular circ*   *suffered from*   *recurrent delusion*   *all women were the Virgin*   *and*   *subject to alternating states of eith*   *utmost clarity or hallucination*   *not well known personally to anyone in Paris except*   *and waiters in*   *Café Mabillon*   *familiar with his figure*   I saw my linotype of thought slugged out, set solid, line for line, justified, page on page, to the typographer's end. I stood rotting and rooted, and something was wrong with my hands that kept dropping the paper. The nails had grown long, curling back to the palm. They were the color of roots. Someone had planted me, I was rooted in the ground. The nails of my
20

toes had burst through the shoes and were growing out and down, curving over the front edges of my shoes. The earth moved, tilting me forward, and I was not dead, I was growing. A woman held her womb open. A cicada cry in her mouth. I was being reborn. Into a thin body this time. And this time I would go somewhere and lead an ideal life. I was in a green wood, in a kind of scrim scene in the background of a stage which was the outside world itself, and it was in that other scene that our real selves were projected and our real lives took place. Someone was combing the fair fields, furrowing them with a great rake, loosening the soil. I was being unlocked from where I grew. The light was growing, everywhere outside, the dawn like milk. I had only to drink. A river of milk, or a river of blood, or a river of bread. It ran under the bridges, down to the sea. A woman held her womb open. I came out. I saw her at the corner of the bridge by the river. She had a branch upraised in her hand. She held flowers out to me as I came over the bridge toward her, surrounded by crying waters. She leaned toward me, extending the flowers. Coquelicots. Breath of flowers. She had high breasts, contrived to offer them. I could not reach that far. Her shadow caught on a tree and fell to the ground and stretched, like a rubber band. A tiny streak of mud ran along one side of it. It was an insoluble problem. It was a long crooked street made of mud and fog, a long series of streets that ran around one side of the world. I was an ancient traveler in that street, mounted on the beast of myself, and I beat my ass with an asphodel but made no progress. I retraced my steps over and through the streets, two steps forward, one step back, I went back over the whole scene, the way it had started.

Back in the beginning. There had been a light in a window. There was a light door, a white face in it, white as the bleached skull of a cow. She turned my bed down. Mother. It was a blue bed, a normal scene. The walls were blue. Sun circled up. She had painted the bedstead blue. It had curly iron ends, with brass balls on top of the corner posts. They shone in the sun, sang in the sun, moved in it, turned like sunflowers. We slept in that bed. It was a universe. Bells rang somewhere, a sweet tongue spoke in my sleep, the brass balls shone. Rang. With light. That street went away, she with it. She went to that place. With a dingdong bell. A slow, low bell, a single bell. Thud. They told me she had gone to that place. They told me she had gone to 'her home.' 'Chez elle,' they called it. She held an asphodel, the brass bell tolled, with a dead sound. At the stroke of twelve. It was I that was struck, at twelve. The brass ball rolled, away. A pawnshop ball. Down the street. It was the sun that rolled and divided the world. It rolled in the street, a fruitstall orange, a red balloon on a straight string, a child's hoop, a ring, a toilet ball, flushed. All faded. I would make my own tumultuous hypotheses in the whirling world, with its bent lenses, its color filters, its mirrors. O she had round paps, soft ones, slim ones. She sang sometimes, beyond the blue bed. Slender-breasted. White pears hanging. I saw her

22

going when she went away. After her, walking in that street, the feet moved over the cobbles, through those hours, years. Followed the walkie-talkie of myself, the movie of existence over which the marquee read QUATRE HEURES DE FOU RIRE, only it was years, not hours, and nobody laughed, everybody was silent. The film had a dumb beginning. Some half-ass poet had invented it all, making up, for square consumption, an imaginary Villon story of lost youth, fabricating romantic goop to fill in the facts nobody knew and which I myself did not remember, adding a narrative voice which was supposed to be myself but was some kind of fourth-person-singular voice I did not recognize, and this nowhere voice began the film by describing an imaginary museum of objects depicting the history of my race, and this museum consisted of one word and one void and one sperm cell in a voiceless pool after the beginning of eternity and one stone forest in the midst of which was chaos and one potential amphibian flopping out of a sea and one polliwog willing to lose its tail and thus establishing the existence of free will and one ape unaware of his essence and one undecided embryo just beginning to represent ontogeny recapitulating phylogeny and one small wooden man looking vaguely like a statue of humanity and vaguely like a statue of inhumanity and one small wooden wheel about to turn and turn and one Greek island adrift in the Aegean and one composite stereopticon illustrating the foetal development of Columbus and one statuesque woman posing as Miss Liberty on a canceled postage stamp and one flower found in Burgundy and pressed in a book in Brooklyn and one wandering Sephardic Jew on the Ellis Island Ferry and one dark French girl in a picture hat having her picture taken by a dark stranger and one picture book showing the sexual motivations of the amateur photographer and one too-hot summer in Brooklyn and one Sephardic construction-worker thirty stories up, transfixed and falling in air, and one still very beautiful woman come back to walk the hills of Burgundy, remembering her girlhood, her blouse full of apples when the sweet birds sang, but I've no further memory of that lost year she died, ten miles from Tonnerre in the Chablis country, although memory is what makes existence continuous and I must certainly have continued somewhere that year I found my fatso self alone in her far country, for I was already none other than myself, Andy Raffine, Brooklyn's baby, turned into an orphan just like that, I was already on the way to becoming myself, I was already in the way of myself wanting to fly or climb, just as there's an ecstatic mechanism in birds that makes them fly upwards in spite of worms, but I was in the wrong country, they told me I was in the wrong country, they sent me back to where I tried to discover Brooklyn in the place I'd left it in memory, I tried to discover myself in the place I'd left myself and her, and we were not where I'd left me, and she was not where she'd left me and night prevented what day allowed as time staggered on through an orphans' home run by a green old couple whose life was over, and then in a cove of Frenchy sisters of a Sacred

24

Heart I picked my pimples through another half a dozen years, and a strange sister said 'You'll be an artist,' and she had a hood that hid gray eyes and she looked at me and a white worm stirred and I started to paint about that time and had nothing to paint but eyes, for souls do not drop into bodies like birds into their reflections although it's their ecstatic mechanisms which really are their souls, and I was trying to climb upward somewhere in the first chapter of my history of climbing and falling, and one night I dreamt a rusty lizard stuck his head in through a one-inch window high in my wall and the world turned and continually renewed itself as I grew and did not renew myself but grew sad wrinkles as I was my son and I was my father not known and not forgotten, and then I was grown out of school at last in a Brooklyn spring in which an odor of patchouli, garlic, and stale beer permeated the premises of a groaning wooden boarding house where I found myself in a rocker on a hot night porch, fanning myself with a newspaper in which was printed the story of everybody's life but my own, and I had been digging myself out of the pit of the centuries to arrive at that rocking moment on the porch in the night of one final Sunday after the War, and then in the next flashed frame of film I see myself bummed back to France and her lost poppy countryside, riding the wooden trains, back and forth, over the autumn country, toothbrush and sketchbook in sack. And ended that year where all trains end, fell out into the Gare Montparnasse, and into a *pension de famille* on the far side of Bastille, and into the Hôtel

Cluny Square another month, and into an attic room on the Ile Saint-Louis another year, and into a high brown room, a high round room in a stone house with a red door in the far end of the Rue Saint-Benoit, and into the Académie Julien, drawing the models, stray hulls of reality, and then so found my own unpaid unplastered place this year behind the Rue du Cherche Midi, my face arrived in a cracked shaving mirror under a bare bulb by a high skylight.

There were wrinkles in the face, already. A fatso face, with little crow's foot wrinkles at the corners of the eyes. Very small ones. As if very small crows had alighted. And flown away almost at once. Yet leaving tracks. They only grew when no one looked. It was just the opposite of the figure in the street. Before I saw her at a corner she was a still life, a still after image, as if of some figure seen and forgotten, but when my eye fell on her she started again to move. Now I remembered her face. Stark, intense, shadowed with what I took for strangeness, it was the same face I had seen in all the pieces of her sculpture exhibited in a small gallery off the Place Saint-Sulpice. Even if I had not first seen her on the sidewalk outside the gallery, I would have known the sculpture was hers. At least I imagined I would have. Even though I saw the face but fleetingly, half-hidden by a kind of cowl. Her eyes were averted, as if intent upon herself, she did not see me as she passed, into the dusk that was always falling. I'd come back to that gallery after that but not seen her there again. Since then, I had glimpsed her only at a distance, in the streets around the Square, each time at a greater distance, at a further remove. Now I was looking for the number of her studio which someone had told me was in the Rue du Cherche Midi, and the number I looked for was the same as my age. That someone was the waiter Lubin at the Café Mabillon. I would simply find the door and knock on it. I would simply say I was a painter and had seen her sculpture in that gallery and wondered if I could see more. Or I might utter some other banality that came into my head. I was looking for that door hidden under the number which was the same as my age in the street that had at least fifty billion houses in it and at least fifty billion doors behind which nested myriad lives, all with their own lips and minds and faces, breasts and hearts, and words and jass and junk and jism spilling out invisible and hot over everything and running out into the gutters and flowing out into the drains and into the sewers and into the rivers under the city and out and down into the sea, the great reservoir of all salt sperm, to be then caught up in clouds and floated away over high lands and dropped down over them so that when it rained the fertile rain fell down on everybody's rooftops and the whole cycle began again, and when the King Fisher was sick the whole world ate Salt Peter and dogs barked at the beaten moon and coffee ran from rooftop gutters, and the fishy king none other than myself, my name a brand of canned salt fish, as I went on spooking around for that ideal number, as if I were looking for a classic coin of a certain dear date, turning over the coins of house

27

numbers in my hand, and myself the fatso hero of that old broken Fatty Arbuckle film that constantly needed rewinding and kept forever slipping off the track. But the true mad hero confronts ever more and more touchingly the world he desires to seize in its entirety, and there is no door with the exact number on it, and the true hero confronts all doors in hunting for the one door behind which sits or hides or lies or waits or meditates his true unmad self. There was no number corresponding exactly to my age in the Rue du Cherche Midi and the street birds forever twittering in the dusk, for in that movie of my wigless self I would not spare myself the falling dusk that made me invisible in a visible world of night through which I moved as on a moving stair until I came to a great square where awnings flapped before the coming of a great rain, and the sky drew up all the air, as dark figures rushed for a last train, throwing themselves into a great hangar of a station with a great god sign that read *Gare Montparnasse,* and the rain came sweeping down the boulevards, sweeping streetwalkers off of them, even as one called from a door and called a name I did not know and meant me, as the rain swept all away before it except a blind man selling goods out of a cardboard box at a side door to the station, and the April rain came down and dripped down from the black brim of his black felt hat into his cardboard box and dripped off his nose and chin, while with a wet horny hand, rather like the pincer of a crab, he wiped a blind eye and heard my step and hawked again what he had in his box, intoning his pitch, listlessly in-

28

toning 'Cravates . . . Lacets . . .' The rain fell down
in loose swirling skeins, the kind a child makes with
string between his fingers. The string was black and fell
tangled like a shadow of itself, dissolving into puddles
that covered the Place Montparnasse in front of the station like backless mirrors from which the gray quicksilver of light still drained. They lay face up all over the
pavement and became, as the last light drained off, windows upon which drummed still more rain. Stray feet
shattered them and fell through, as if through eyes of
earth. Or as into blind mouths. And the rain fell all
night along the boulevards and into the bent side streets
and onto the roofs and into the eaves of the earth, and
ran in the drains with a coffee sound as the wind came
up again in breathing gusts, and light at last fell down
in place of rain and dawn came down with sperm of
light on a thousand toits as I still wandered round about
and through that street that wound around the world
that year among the imaginary dancers.

And this was
the Rue du Cherche Midi, a short street, despite its long
name in search of itself, in which I was a young astrono-
mer looking for some meridian, searching the south and
the center and the noon of myself, and this street ran
shortly into the Rue de Vaugirard which was the longest
street in Paris and which began at the Sorbonne and
passed the Luxembourg Gardens and went on across the
Boulevard Raspail and across the Rue de Rennes and
past Montparnasse and across the Boulevard Pasteur
and past the Porte de Versailles and on and on and on,

and back. Only at dawn it left me off at the Rue du Cherche Midi where the door to my place had a number close to my age. I fell in, up the winding stair, lay down in drunk daylight under the eaves, slept and dreamt in the dark of it.

It was the quicksilver dark at the back of a mirror, and the number of my door had been close to the number of my years, and thus *her* door was close by, perhaps in the same block, perhaps in the next building where there were skylights too. Her studio, on the other side of these walls. I would hear her voice through these walls, even if I had never heard it awake. I recognized her now, saw her, imagined her, that 'classic face,' strange coif of hair, sweet tit. In the semi-dark. In the great place of my sleep where sperm of light still fell. De-silvered mirrors lay about, face up, each a window, and these windows no longer blind. Each was an open eye on myself, each revealed a part of me, each a window in the house of myself. It was a tall, tall house. But, inside, all the floors had been taken out, so that my pudgy fat body filled up the frame of the house from basement to roof. My body filled every corner of it, I was a huge balloon of a man, similar to one of those huge blown-up figures in carnival parades, swaying and tottering in the sky. The walls of my body pressed against the walls of my house at all points. Why was I so fat? I sweated too much, the walls of the building sweated, like the concierge's little fat pig-dog that panted and sweated and had one blind eye and panted and sweated and barked and blinked and rolled over on

30

the cobbles outside the concierge's cubicle. Every morning the little fat dog was there, sunning itself on the cobbles, and panting and blinking and sweating and rolling over with its blind eye on the sky, a real *chien d'Andalou*. I felt a little pain in the lower regions. Something like a straightened-out inner tube was blown up too tight inside of me. I wanted to release a little air from it, and there was no valve. But if the partitions all had been taken out inside of me, if all the walls inside had been taken out, then all I had to do was to let air out at any point and the pressure would be relieved all over. I could let some air out of the upper windows just as well as below, and the whole swelling would go down. The whole swelling of myself. The windows were not all open, as I had supposed. They were all filled with the glass of mirrors from which the quicksilver had run off. But there was one that was free, one I could look through. My sleeping, seeing-eye could see.

                     In the house that had no walls, I could see her studio, up under the eaves and skylights, at the top of that yellow building. Unfinished wet clay statues stood about, like ghosts in their wet canvas shrouds. A parrot in a corner said Yawk, turned twice about, baleful, muttering, fixed the intruder with a blind stare, myself, come in, through a ruined wall, invisible. Odor of incense and rose leaves mingled with the powdered smell of clay, suggesting the musty underground smell of the church of Saint-Julien-le-Pauvre. A faint smell of parrot-droppings recalled the offerings of irreverent church pigeons. In the back,

31

on a narrow couch over which two candles guttered, amid an accumulation of smocks and towels, she lay. I had been looking for her for a long time in the street of the earth, I had come home nowhere save where her traces were. A normal delusion. A brass ball whirled in the sky, tossed and whirled, whirled and tossed, like a heavy autumn leaf. It circled up, fell into gold, speechless canals. She was unaware, in the semi-dark of that studio. She was one of her own statues which, failing as stone, had come to life in flesh, the skin like smooth plaster, the face contemplative in its stillness, shadowed by its dark cowl of hair. Or it was no more than a still, dumb face, white as the bleached forehead of a cow's skull, to which I imputed the illusion of contemplation, a dummy I dressed in my own imaginings. She was not undressed, nor asleep. There was someone else in the room, someone who moved about in the dim light in a far corner. This someone was putting a record on an old wind-up phono. The music started, the person I could not see came back toward where she lay on the couch. She lay listening with a calm bemused satisfaction, as if the music almost but not quite confirmed something she had already long known. Pan with a pipe blew in a bosky place. A dead Pan, a horny classical pipe. I could see only her unfinished statues where they stood about in the suspended light. Her statues resembled each other in a certain characteristic spareness, a seeming unwillingness to cover the armature and skeleton of being. Each one of her statues resembled her, unfinished, half-realized, half-comprehended images of herself, and the image of herself was in the music. A fluted line hung in air, curled inward upon itself, fell, like a piece of curled white string. It fell into shadows, silence and darkness. Hours passed, for the shadows shifted, turned upon themselves in the breathing silence, a silence filled with what I took for the breath of lovers on the dark of the couch. Or a wind at a window. Wind whirred at a window, a white gauze curtain blew in, the parrot, muttering, turned twice about on its pedestal. Then she was alone on her couch, as I was alone in my sleep, and when one is alone one tells onself true sad stories, and I was telling myself such a tale, over and over, always the same.

The tale of myself, located somewhere between a picnic and the sea, where I walked leaving fossil footprints. Stars went dead during the day, but there was still Fatso Raffine, not so refined, trying to refine himself. I was refining myself, going over my fat dead, my several selves mislaid, each abandoned in the midst of some sequence of gesture, as if the movie projectionist had suddenly run off amok to another camera loaded with later images of the same self. The movie projectionist had been afflicted by a form of demented praecox in which he lost all interest in the objects and people before him on the screen, for the portrait of the hero as a real drag was a real drag to everyone but the hero himself, and the film dragged, and the projectionist rushed into the streets to embrace the first person he met who could laugh or love, while my organ had turned into the voice of those who wept. And I saw her

33

statues now, in that studio, for what they were. Each one of them represented an image in one of my own paintings, an image I had seldom or never realized as central to the painting, often no more than a fleeting figuration in a flowing background between two strokes of paint, and each statue became larger than life, each still growing, swelling like the huge balloons of statues in street parades. It kept swelling up, and pressed against the sides of the building and up against the skylights, finally bursting through them into the high sky, and the huge tottering figure waved in the sky with that strange animation of inanimate material when made into animal form, like the fat dummy of a dog, and the form worked loose from its moorings and shot up into the air, drifting out over the Paris skyline, only suddenly to leak air like water, like a fat dog pee-ing, and wither in an instant and fall into the streets of the city where it lay on the pavements like knotted rubber bands. All the images of myself did the same, all the statues escaped through the skylights, and all over the city they were finding heaps of curious rubber bands and curled pieces of string on the streets and sidewalks, choking the gutters. It was a plague of rubber bands and string, and there was no use for them even in quantity, for they were all just slightly used or soiled, and not long enough to wrap around anything. It was the string I used to steal and hoard. No one recognized the white string for what it was, no one recognized it as the shriveled armature of that primal nude figure which hid in all statues, public and private, and in everyone's clothes as they

34

walked down the street. They passed their own statues on pedestals, the hand in the vest, and did not recognize themselves for what they were, like people perpetually too unhappy in themselves ever to read anything but happy stories or see films with sweet endings. They would call the cops to have the exhibitors of such films arrested. They would call the streetcleaners to have the unsightly plague of pure string carted away before it got light in the morning and everybody saw themselves and recognized themselves for the first time. They were still coming after me, to arrest me for my childhood thefts, the string I'd tried to collect. That string had been pure white. I knew for sure it was pure white. I had only to possess her body now to know it.

I saw her as a creature entirely alone, her naked body not strange and classic in its unrelievable loneliness, but simply unfinished, incomplete. Spring shook wings in me, a cool perfume clung to her, drawing me down to her with the force of a physical gesture, and I had only, I had only fully to awaken her, had only to bring her to a new awareness, to an ecstasy she had not yet known, and her eyes closed as I came over her, her arms went about me, her lips opened under mine, her tongue came hot in my mouth, and wind whirred at a window, two candles guttered and went out, and I had not heard the music stop, and she pressed my head down, down, as I kissed her throat, the hollows at the base of it, the swelling where her breasts began, and still she pressed me down, pressed her breast to my lips, moaning, still pressed me down, and I kissed her thighs, but she wanted my lips again, drew me upward again, and she, and she a sweet strange vessel, she an anonymous vessel, an anonymous receptacle into which I could pour myself, pour the history of myself without words, the act of love its own adequate eloquence, and yet, and yet somewhere, and yet somewhere near the memory of the unimaginable, a wood cross guarded the passes, the free sea-sluices. Someone had erected a turnstile, and it was necessary to drop coins in the slotted box at the gate, if you were a virgin. The way had remained open only as long as our thin fictions, we existed only as long as our fictions, and I was much too fat to enter, and guided only by those who were thinner than myself I could not pass the gate through which they went so easily. I noticed it was not only the fat ones such as myself who could not get through. All sorts of others existed in that curious world on my side of the gates. And there were other kinds of gates that many seemed to slip through. Everyone was playing some kind of night-game in which I had only to learn the rules, in which I had only to identify the players. Rapt players rose from gaming tables and staggered off over a horizon of deserted park benches and abandoned rowboats that knocked together as a lighthouse cast its megaphone over the sea. Two lone figures emerged from the sea, wearing dilapidated clothes. They might have been men and they dragged an enormous wardrobe filled with more dilapidated clothes which they persuaded themselves were a priceless treasure. They persuaded others

36

that their trunk contained priceless treasures, and they
formed governments to distribute them, but as soon as
the citizens of the world donned those priceless clothes,
the legs and arms of the garments immediately began
running and crawling and jumping back to the ocean,
and threw themselves back into it, carrying the people
inside of them to their deaths. It was only when one of
their number freed himself from his clothing of fat flesh
that he was able to escape, and the few that did escape
did not swim back to the land but seaward toward new
ships, which they never reached, for these ships had
now become streamlined vehicles moving at high
speeds over all the Route One seaways and highways
of the earth, and the two original figures that might
have been women were now trapped in a desolate landscape made of paper cutouts of country houses, terrible
nutless animals, and jewelry spouting out of the heads
of fashion models. The two fat figures which might have
been a man and a woman had in the course of their
wanderings become married to each other, but mon-
strous strontium mutations had taken place in each of
them so that neither knew any longer which part he or
she was to play, and both thumbed eternally through
college catalogues, reading over and over the names of
courses designed to reteach the emotions of love. They
now found themselves in a dancehall jungle and each
was forced to dance separately with Andalusian dogs
dressed up like the family portraits of dogs seen in bar-
bershop posters. They were all wearing loose Saint
Louis shoes, strangely like a pair of shoes I myself once

owned, and each had been asked by his beloved to bring his mother's heart as food for his lover. Red hearts were preferred for dog food, and one of the lovers tore out the heart of his mother, stumbled up with it, dropped it on the dancefloor before the other, and the heart rolled over gasping 'Are you hurt, my son?'

Shot sun winged to zenith, plummeted, into the outrageous abyss on the other side of day. Streetlights came out in it, and I was no longer with her in that strange studio of a dancehall. I was going somewhere to my own funeral, through the late dusk that kept falling and falling. I had fallen from that place where she was, and my face upon the face of the street had grown old in falling, become happier, no good. I had fallen from her, fallen away from her, and falling, falling through the speechless air, all fell with me, statues, towers, buildings, battlements, all down, all gone in soundless light. Yet she went ahead of me through the streets, wearing a kind of a cape, walking as if blind, intent upon herself. Or upon others not present. Or others I could not see. She existed in a different world, yet we passed within a calling of each other through the Place Saint-Sulpice and up the Allée du Séminaire with its fake ruins and classic columns holding up nothing. Old men sat on wood benches among demented pigeons in the dark, and at the Luxembourg Gardens, where that Allée came to a broken end, the gates were already locked for the night. Unreal Paris with its closed gardens alive in the night engulfed the figure I'd followed, her body passed through the
38

iron fencing of the gardens, her dreamed body went through, mine caught clumsy fat outside, my head upon a picket, turning, spitted. Her form moved among the flowered trees of the park where the contemplative statues stood about, tranquil dames in stained marble. She stood still, she was one of them. She had her hand extended, she seemed to be feeding the other statues, like birds. A cat came out along the stone wall below the iron pickets, rubbing its arched back against them. I reached for it and saw her eyes. They looked nearsighted. This was why she never noticed me following, never recognized me, wondering who I was, perhaps saw only a fat blob on the landscape. Disdainful, hunching a little, the cat scooted back through the railings. In the hushed dark of the park, reality and illusion mixed. A dialogue of statues. A bird with wings of stone, turning twice about, flew off its pedestal. Another cat, or the same, went sleepwalking under the trees. The trees had the look of loving, the night an extraordinary drunkenness, as of summer dusks. I could no longer see the statue with its hand extended. She had slipped off in the shadows of the park, while I still stood in the Rue de Vaugirard. The pewter street moved under me, an escalator with an iron fence for a railing, and I moved forward along the moving fence, past dark figures pressed together, stick figures stuck together in the world's end, holding each other, against dark walls. How had the lonely met? A complicated music, involving all space and time, had hung them together in that time and place. Where the Rue de Vaugirard was narrow, passing over to the Boulevard Saint-Michel, there was hidden laughter, muffled music behind closed shutters. Behind the blinds a desultory music probed some sweet initial wound, or so I imagined, seeing myself a body on a bed behind those shutters, with a laughing face that might have been mine, and with someone else there, a girl, not laughing, looking down, stuffing out a cigarette beside the bed. Perhaps there was only a girl by herself behind those shutters, playing the phonograph, only a street wall between us, nothing really separating us, her door no more than a screen between us in some schizophrenic hospital we were all in, and the two of us, all of us, all splintered parts of the same whole. I liked to imagine she was looking for her other half, that she would lean out, opening the shutters, see me going by. It was an old fantasy. 'She' did nothing of the kind. Further along, two more figures stuck in a doorway. The man had her up against the stone of the entrance, pressing into her, her head back against the stone, her eyes closed. He was so short that the top of his head came only to the base of her throat, his face buried in it as he pressed against her. He was so fat that his body completely enveloped hers, engulfed it, like an amoeba surrounding its food. He fed on her, and he was as fat as myself, almost, and just as I came past, her eyes half-opened, looked across over his head, met my eyes and held them, and I was he, and she whispering 'Noel . . . Noel. . . .' She kept calling me Noel, still looking in my eyes, and she kept whispering my name over and over, and my eyes kept telling her it was not Noel, and it made no difference, I was still Noel, and the fat body of the actual man that was pressing her against the wall was not named Noel either, for he too had had to settle for an identity she had laid on him, just as everyone else he knew had laid *their* identities on him, and she could say nothing but Noel . . . Noel, because it *was* Noel and she could not lie, and still I would stop those words and names behind which everyone hid and was hidden and that were the buildingblocks of false identities. The instant of my passing was all that was needed to accomplish it. The message of my eyes was a tongue stopping her tongue, my eyes were lips stopping her lips with kisses that were keys, and this was but the start of it, and I had another skeleton key, lower down, which I could insert in her keyhole, to turn the love of her. Her hair was straw, her name was Heidi. There were six flowers in her garden. I picked the petals off all six flowers to prove what I wanted to believe. She loved me not. She loved me. And her eyes said to me: 'It is different in my country. It is too warm there for people to die.' And she closed her eyes and went back to her own country, losing me in the Noel she still imagined pressed against her, into her.

Polyglot, loud with babeled tongue, the Boulevard Saint-Michel rocked in the night, came awake in the dark of it. A nightmaze upon me, among the sidewalk terraces and students and street arabs and sidewalk photographers and cronies hawking combs and bearded Chinese, East Indians, Moroccans, Senegalese, Americans and Germans with cameras, sailors and waiters and Noels without names and strolling cops in capes. I fell through the pouring crowd in which 'she' was lost. Downhill. Fleeting. At the eternal corner where the Boulevard Saint-Germain cut across Saint-Michel, by the tall iron gates of the Cluny Gardens, a band of three violinists, each with his cup, fiddled disparately. The separate, screeching strands of music fell upon the curled iron gates and wound about them like snapped violin strings or rubberbands, only to dissolve immediately in the carnival sound of the street. Just inside the wrought gates, three silent stone-winged griffons sat in darkness, unmoved. A parade of some sort was forming in front of the Café DuPont Latin. One hundred and ninety-three student Moroccans and Algerians had begun a snake-dance on its terrace, singing and stamping and hollering and waving placards reading *Tout Est Con Chez DuPont* while a jukebox jumped inside, and the whirling line of black figures caught up stray nursemaids, Beaux Arts students, dance instructors, visiting tourist dowagers, streetwalkers, Sorbonne professors, girls with books and flowers, and carried them off screaming in a stomping dance, winding down the boulevard and past the stone silent griffons and across the intersection and smack into the middle of a sidewalk fair of colored striped tents and barkers and shooting galleries and miniature ferris wheels and Guignol booths and barking dogs and hurdy-gurdy players, and just as the snake-dance line ran into the streetfair crowd a wailing wild ragged band of American poets from the Rue Git-le-Coeur rushed out of a side street into the

42

middle of the boulevard and fell into the winding line, jumping onto the shoulders of the dancers and hanging onto the necks of the women, singing and shouting that the Poetry Police were coming to save them, the Poetry Police were coming to save them all from death, Captain Poetry was coming to save the world from itself, to make the world safe for beauty and love, the Poetry Police had arrived to clean up the mass mess, the Poetry Police were about to descend in parachutes made from the pages of obscene dictionaries, the Poetry Police were about to land simultaneously in the central squares of forty-two major cities, having chartered all the planes in the world and being furnished with free seats for an endless passage since all were *poids net,* the Poetry Police were about to land simultaneously on the tops of the tallest buildings and bridges and monuments and fortifications of the world and take complete command of the rapidly deteriorating world situation, the Poetry Police were about to invade Geneva and decide once and for all what the shape of the table should be at all future peace conferences, the Poetry Police were about to consolidate their positions simultaneously in all parts of the world by climbing onto the backs and hanging onto the necks of everyone and shouting true profound wiggy formulas for eternal mad salvation, the Poetry Police were about to capture all libraries, newspapers, printing presses, and automats, and force their proprietors at pen's point to print nothing henceforth but headlines of pure poetry and menus of pure love, every day's papers to be filled with nothing henceforth

43

but pure poetry stories giving the latest positions and poses and appearances and manifestations and demonstrations of pure beauty made out of the whole cloth of naked reality itself as well as the latest reports on the latest actions of love throughout the universe, publishing all the love that was fit to print and all the love that was not fit to print but refusing to publish any stories or headlines or pictures on any other subject at all since no other subject was News any more, and even the great unretouchable editors of Death Magazine in their high glass offices would raise their venetian blinders and I was *poids net* Andalous Raffine, I was Andy Raffine reduced to net weight, and I was riding lightly on the shoulders of an enormous black thrush in black tights with a headdress like the Statue of Liberty and a flaming torch in her hand which she waved about setting fire to the tailcoats of real policemen, functionaries, politicians, legionnaires, and clergymen, and I on top of her picking feathers from her Statue of Liberty headdress which was made of real American pigeon feathers, and these Soul-feathers I dipped in the light of blazing electric streetlamps, and with my feather brush thus dipped wrote great blazing paintings on secondstory walls running the length of every street, and with my feather pen thus dipped wrote great blazing poems on unwinding toilet paper, and these great endless mad poems I draped across the streets and boulevards, from streetlamp to streetlamp, and dropped them in swirls around the heads of elderly civilians who gobbled them up, fought over them, and rushed home to paste them up on shaving mirrors and on union barberpoles and on the walls of union warehouses and on the backsides of the Chamber of Deputies, the Conciergerie, the Opéra and the Opéra Comique and the Cirque Medrano where circling circus horses and their standing bareback riders read them and fell down rapt but singing in the sawdust, as well as on the front walls of every American Express and every suburban apartment building in the outskirts of all cities and on the side doors of all churches and temples, with the word Love underlined wherever it occurred in a poem, and the Poetry Revolution was growing, the Poetry Revolution was shaking, transforming existence and civilization as it rolled down around the corner of the Boule Miche and down the Boulevard Saint-Germain toward Odéon where Danton watched over a Metro entrance and pocket-watches hung from trees each with a different time swinging in the breeze but all of them indicating it was later than you think, while crowds of black berets and herds of sandals came floating and staggering and flying out of the Café Mabillon and the Pergola to join the much-belated Poetry Revolution, while three thousand nine hundred and forty-two alumni of the Académie Duncan came streaming out of the Rue de Seine combing their hair with Grecian lyres. And the original small band of mad poets scattering true apocalyptic visions was lost and drowned in the swelling parade of humanity and inhumanity that carried within it all the places of its exile, and the long-delayed parade of true and final flippy Liberation went bowling along past the cafés at the carrefour of Saint

45

Germain-des-Près where the original two deaf and dumb mad monkeys of the Café des Deux Magots leaped at last off their eternal chained pedestals and onto my back as I still rode lightly along, but now I was on the shoulders of no black thrush, I was on the back of a great black horse instead, I was on the back of Horse itself, I was on Horse, and Horse flew, as the snowballing mob of liberated man rolled on down the boulevard toward unconquered territory, pausing briefly for the absorption of Jean-Paul Sartre and his flies, and Albert Camus and his rebels, and James Joyce and his blooms, and Pablo Picasso and his harlequins and horses and blueplates and Guernicas and doves, and Céline with Henry Miller in his pocket, and Fernand Léger with feet caught in a machine, and Antonin Artaud and his mother, and René Char and his bad boys, and Michel Mourre and his dead God in an Easter pulpit, and Marc Chagall on *his* Horse, and Samuel Beckett and his unnamable selves, and their ranks further augmented by hundreds if not thousands of holdout members of underground Resistance movements, hundreds if not thousands of Maquis who had still been hidden waiting for decades in backstreet caves all over the Left Bank, waiting for the true Liberation that they still believed had yet to arrive, but who now came bursting out of scores of sidestreets and throwing worn sniper slingshots away fell forward into the moving flood of humanity that erected signs and placards and streamers as it went proclaiming amnesty to all who had wronged sweet humanity during the prolonged Occupation of the world, circulating handbills

46

in every passing building and courtyard and café and store instructing all backward and still doubting elements of the populace that all they had to do was now surrender their weapons of doubt and throw in their arms and all would be forgiven, and the gutters began to be flooded with old machine guns, daggers, and pistolets thrown from surrendering windows, but still there were coalmen with carts and plumbers and salesmen and ward politicians and suspended windowcleaners who threw down their own particular kind of arms and shouted blessings and hurrahs when they saw the signs of Peace and Love but as soon as the signs were out of sight immediately turned back to beating their children and wives and mothers and mothers-in-law, whereas as soon as the Seine was crossed onto the Right Bank which was the wrong bank a strange change in the atmosphere and spirit of things was immediately evident, for the great parade first-off ran smack into a solid cordon of nine thousand mercenaries, Royalists, and gendarmes who ringed the Place de la Concorde and roped off the gardens of the Tuileries and the Louvre and the Champs Elysées, presenting a solid front of startled, hastily formed opposition to the new spontaneous movement of Love, and now newly startled citizens jumped up out of their pants and ran away up every street at the first sight of the oncoming placards, and all the sitters in the grand cafés on the Champs Elysées, hearing the still oncoming hordes, looked suddenly down upon themselves and found themselves nude and jumped up, without paying for their *consommations,* and ran for their lives, just as I who would say I no more was trampled underfoot in the surging throngs, and my death had come from falling underfoot from a high place, and as I fell between a zero and the infinite I tried to stop myself just long enough to accomplish one significant action in my life, as a dying person says Just wait one moment more, I'm not quite ready, I have one more important thing I want to do, if you'll just wait, but after birth there was only one significant action left and that was the action of dying itself, and I had been somewhere on a long journey into Piblokto madness and I had ridden Horse for three days through Lapland and I had seen the junkie midnight sun and fed cloth mushrooms to terrible reindeers who trampled me forever underfoot and slipped my body through a crack in eternity. A horse stood over my bed, looking down at me, and Horse's mouth opened and colored brains fell out as moths and telephones buzzed. I fell away and fell and fell and fell where pigeons-turned-to-waterbirds cawed and cawed. I was trying to unhitch my parachute. It had a secret catch, a final insoluble secret. It had not opened in time and lay tangled about me. I had been too heavy for it, for the parachute of my skin, and as I was falling a priest had been paddling by, a mad cyclist in the sky, pedaling furiously upward. He kept pedaling past me as I fell, leaning out with a kind of a hook, the kind that windowcleaners use on ledges, to catch me. But he did not. Horse had left me flat, and now I lay trying to unhitch my parachute that had never opened. The final hearses of my imagination trundled through my sleep, a sleep which I had imagined to be the sleep of death. Even as I awoke, the priest on the bicycle kept circling round me, pedaling back and forth, in and out of reality. Some cock cried out kikiriki as if it were morning, some cock was fooling himself that it was morning back on earth, making it easy for me to fool myself that I was none other than myself again, having not escaped my skin, waking up as usual in my own place in the Rue du Cherche Midi.

             I had not fallen as far as I thought. One end of me had been tied down someplace, and I had stretched like a rubber band, but now had snapped back in place, with my face in the cracked shaving mirror beneath a bare bulb under the high skylight. The same meat face. Only the crows had lighted on my face again and this time walked about more extensively, leaving larger and deeper tracks than before. They looked less like crow's tracks and more like pigeon's tracks now. It was almost as if they had been looking for something, their tracks crossing and recrossing my forehead like a recurrent thought. Or like an obsessive idea, back and forth, furrowing my brainpan, raking it, as if with a very small pocketcomb. I was combing my hair in front of the cracked mirror. The cracks in the mirror had grown while no one was looking, but it was the same mirror, the same hole in the wall through which I could still see her studio. In reality a tiny hole, such as comes from pulling a long nail or a sliver of lathing out of the plaster. Outside the sun fell off the roof, dusk's yellow skin drew over, someone put

49

the night's umbrella up. A night-tent, full of moth holes. Vision of toiletpaper clouds, unrolling, pot visions of cosmic moons, crepe-paper suns in the night. A thin face in it, and a body, swimming, in and out of reality. Swimming away, but not too fast, as if half-willing to be caught. Then who was it put the tits on backwards? Lack-love like that, too hard to play. Ask the waiter Lubin, he knew all, the layman's confessor, he could tell. He had told me already. His mouth moved over the story, through it. It was he who would tell me the true story of myself, and it had all happened a long time ago. He was one of those people who always talked as if everything that had ever happened to anyone had already happened to him. Just start to tell him about it, he'd nod his head, and tell *you*. His tongue moved in his mask, the phono went round, the libretto of the story spilled out, like a ham opera, your story, her story, everybody's story. He had told me her studio was next to where I lived. Or I thought he had. I had seen her through the hole, now saw her again. There was someone with her again, coming toward her, kissing her hair, her throat, her breasts. Mouth on mouth. She made a small moaning, did not hear the music stop. Wind whirred, curtains blew, candles guttered and went out, hours of absinthe passed. I had a bottle by myself, drank it by myself, everything funny and strange, a wiggy carrousel, turning and turning. Smoke rings turned to rings of words I reached for like the brass rings on a merry-goround. The phono went round, the absinthe acted. Floating about four feet above myself, I looked down

50

and saw myself a liberated spirit holding a glass that had turned to a toad. And it broke like a burst of laughter. Each time I looked through the hole it was the same, over and over. The phono, someone coming toward her, the wind, the curtain, the statues glimpsed again. But the scene did change, it was not I that changed. Each time there was something different about her statues, each time there was something different about her. Parts of the statues were missing, a hand here, an arm there, fallen. Each time it was a different lover and each time the statues of herself were further dismembered. Now all without arms. The parrot on its pedestal, muttering, turned twice about, flew away into the dark back of the studio, alighted on the floor near one statue, found an eye rolling, took the eye up in its beak, flew up, out through the skylight. I had not heard the phono stop, and time ran on through its egg cup. Her hair had a woody smell. I was drunk in the dark of it. Her lips were not illusion, her breasts not white doves. Souls did not nest in them, although a tiny wood cross lay between them, on a transparent thread. I kissed her breasts, a pulse beat everywhere in me, my body filled with an intolerable singing ache. Neither was that illusion. I kissed the inside of her legs, her thighs, and she drew me up, fastened her mouth to mine, made a small moaning in her throat. A beam of light fell suddenly from the skylight, reflected from a passing car, onto her statues where they lay about, dismembered. Arms, heads, eyes, mouths, lips, blind breasts, all fallen. Love itself had fallen away in the anonymous, was carried

51

away in pieces, the beast remained. Or so I imagined, so I thought. I fell away, alone in my place.

Except I was never alone. Even when I had stacked my paintings away, turning them all against the walls, as they now were stacked, they were waiting there, unspeakably demanding. There they all were still, all chimeras, chiaroscuro illusions, dead stick figures I had yet to bring to real life. I'd begin over. And I had a brush for a tongue, and the brush made flesh, no need to dip it in a paintpot, my hand itself the brush with the endless fleshpot of my body tied to it and draining into it a bottomless reservoir of funky flesh from which ran boiling rivers of arteries spilling out their umbered pigments upon the canvas ground where formed the limbs the figures the faces of a drunken longing, and not all human, for there were yearning dogs and hungry horses' heads among them, and I had not heard the music stop, wailing with a funky face the found soul of things, not able to hold it, holding it, beating it, whirling the paint on canvas, sugar of air on tongue turned to body's salt, the skull with ears on it, liquid porches, spilling light, onto the canvas, pools of it forming into shape of eyes, the eyes that I would look into, but as soon as they were formed they ran down as with too much turpentine and ran onto the longing dogs and horses and turned into echoes of laughter with every mocking sound a different color echoing about the canvas and transfiguring all its painted parts, horses' penises turned to yellow flutes which fitted to manifolds which fitted into female

52

plumbing which in turn dissolved and floated down nearest streets as yellow sunlight while umbered shadows melted and percolated up into the gutters of tilted houses in one of which I now slept amazed at the marvelous miraculous painting I was doing with every stroke a master stroke of the purest genius and never a stroke to be painted over, the very soul of liberated creation itself, except that I had trouble with one thing, I still had trouble painting eyes, I had yet to paint eyes that had the look of undreamy reality in them, I had yet to paint 'her' with clear eyes, and each time some dark hooded romantic figure raised up its head I painted it out with one great stroke and banished it and kept on painting the face of creation, that creation which shouted and sang and whispered and wailed and ate and slept and lay down and was sad after intercourse and got up again and put another record on and looked out the window and saw something still uncaptured on the far side of the street and years later or minutes later went to find it or tried to capture it in painting, and all I painted turned into one huge landscape of flesh, all the canvases laid end on end became a continuous landscape of bone and flesh, one awakened body to which I made love in the flesh of paint, but when I came to paint her eyes they were closed, and when I painted them open they were blank, without pupils, staring, for the thing that replaced the romantic was the void of existence itself, or the secret of it, and if I could imagine the true expression of those eyes I would have articulated that final irreducible secret, while for a year I had wandered in the depopulated world of the non-objective trying to paint in the abstract what could never be captured in paint, for lead and linseed oil and pigment were themselves things and by their nature not abstract, and any non-objective image made with them inescapably an illusion or hallucination of some sort, and thus I began painting over all my old canvases, one after the other, laying on a continuous concrete city of yellow houses with womblike windows and doors which seemed at first as if they would never open again, as if the houses were forever shut and tenantless or at best but temporarily rented by summer-people always away, yet I was opening those doors, prying them open again with a palette knife in one hand and a painting knife in the other, and laying on so many new open windows that the buildings became all open windows with humans falling and jumping out of them, all the lost figures of that depopulated land came tumbling out, the liberated images of desire sprung again upon the canvas-ground like hungry sensual animals too long locked separately away but now falling upon each other in attitudes of love and devouring each other's bodies and legs and insatiable lips from which hot tongues forked and licked and sucked until all their fleshpaint fused into one body of loving at a seething center of existence where a great wind blew, and the great wind that blew through all my paintings was the force of life itself which, like some huge bicycle pump, blew its breath into the inner tube of every vessel it found at hand, and these blown-up figures moved with gigantic steps

54

through a gigantic reality, encompassing fantastic existences, unimaginable lives, never-realized civilizations in which the citizens sat at gaming tables perpetually playing for unimaginable stakes, and these gaming tables like the stone chess and checker tables in Washington Square or the Luxembourg Gardens at which young adventurers with spears turned into old bent men as they played, and the carved figures they moved on their boards were ships that put out constantly for lost shores in sea limbos where still swam the untamed creatures of original animal existence, a forgotten and still-to-be rediscovered ferment of original sperm upon which still sailed rafts loaded with seven-foot men with one-foot penises, and these rafts continually boarded by swimming hordes of women with musk flowers in their hair who waded naked into the sea from their bound, trussed-up shores to climb aboard the great rafts and lash the crew to the decks and masts and climb on top of them and exhaust them in perpetual orgasm, at which point they threw the men fainting into the sea to revive them and then jumped down upon them in the water and rode them coupled in coitus to those shores in the far beginning of the world where I would still capture them in paint.

I was having an orgasm in paint, but at the very climax of that Action Painting a strange thing began to happen. There was a little nowhere bird trying with his beak to tie a little string around my panting, painting member, trying to bring me down. That stranger little bird wound a wiggy little horn in me and sounded with his axe to see if he could bring me down and shut my sexy phoenix song. He was in my pants, he was gnawing on my lowest bone. My clothes were too tight for me but my pants were too big for him. The voice of the bird was too big for him, too small for me. The voice of the bird was a tight voice, and he tied me up, and his beak was the needle of a phono scratching an old broken tune, with its melody like a lost inhabitant threading his way up and down back stairs in my building, closing and opening doors, coming and going on wooden stairs that spiraled up and up, and the night made of lost doors closing and opening and closing again on all women I'd ever known, and the doors closing on each room as I left it, and each room of my life with a door that had closed and the handle fallen off, and each person a door that had closed, so that I now saw them all coming and passing and going away through hotel doors and backyard doors cellar doors screen doors kitchen doors boardinghouse doors classroom doors and doors to parlors subways bathrooms restrooms poolrooms paintrooms studios and doors to all the streets I'd ever lived in run together into one long narrowing street in perfect classic perspective with the lines of the curbs always growing closer and closer together but never meeting, while that phono-bird still ground its beak, faster and faster, then slower and slower, but over and over the same broken tune. But the record was my own head going around, and the beak of that bird had grooved my skull, and that phono had two old-fashioned horn-type speakers which were my ears

in the end of that narrowing street with its classic lines
of perspective that never quite came together anywhere
as I kept walking into that perspective, following 'her'
fleeting figure which was always about to disappear
over the horizon which itself was always vanishing and
growing further and further away. For my feet were
made of unbaked clay pressed into the kind of boots
with heavy leads on their bottoms that deepsea divers
wear, while at every corner I passed an old blind man
in a black felt hat offering rubber shoelaces and laughing hideously, and in the middle of every block as I
went on I came upon some kind of group of crazy drunk
people who blocked my path without seeming to see me
or to be conscious of me as they shouted and laughed
and gesticulated to each other, and in one block there
was a bunch of celebrating officials in official robes of
state, and in the next block was a knot of singing policemen, and in the next a knot of mumbling priests, and in
the next a squad of American soldiers in dress uniforms
marching in impenetrable formation in lock-step ten
abreast from building-to-building in the constantly narrowing street while a commander in boxer shorts with
a German camera slung behind him led them with an
ebony baton singing verses from an Armed Forces
Guide to an Endless Occupation with a special intro-
duction signed if not written by the General of the
Combined Allied Forces and the President of the USA,
said guide ending with the reminder that although
Fraternization was not against the U.S. Constitution
and Bill of Rights nevertheless it should be remembered

by all naïve soldiers about to debark on German soil that our final objective was the complete and final annihilation of all enemy forces, through all of which I goofed onward, having to dodge up alleys and through windows to avoid being trampled beneath the oblivious or seemingly oblivious groups going in the opposite direction, and with each block the groups grew larger until in the middle of each block there was a regular mob blocking my path, some in formation and some in angry fist-shaking knots, but all of them increasingly organized, seemingly to block my advance toward that disappearing figure on the horizon, and scattering various kinds of printed manifestoes and regulations and protocols and codes and restrictions and taboos and constitutions and traffic regulations and accepted maxims and venerated proverbs for the sane conduct of civilized society as it had always been wisely conducted by great statesmen and recognized elders who knew by hard business experience how common sense prudence providence cleanliness regular habits and hardwork were the virtues which would always triumph, proving in the end that it paid in dollars and cents to be trustworthy loyal helpful friendly courteous kind obedient cheerful thrifty brave clean and reverent. But something that was not red paint but a parody of paint was running in the gutter, and it was not water, although as far as I could tell nobody had noticed it, and I was too occupied with my own private pursuits to say to them Pardon me but did you happen to notice your feet have some kind of liquid blackjack gum stuck to them, Par-

don me I think you must have stepped on something, or
in something, whichever way you want to look at it,
something which I hope you will not mistake for *caca
du chien* for it has a more reddish color and in fact
resembles sticky blood more than anything, Yes it is embarrassing the way it sticks and won't wash off and I
hope you will pardon me for intruding on you to mention it but I thought you might possibly like to know
that the human color of it fascinated me, could not help
but fascinate me since I'm a painter, if you will excuse
the aberration, if you will excuse the uncomely conduct
and the unseemly conduct as well as the intrusion into
your high affairs and deliberations, but perhaps you will
understand, perhaps you will be understanding in view
of the circumstances and not prosecute, because that
running substance was rising and even getting into my
paint brushes and even onto my canvases which would
all be completely ruined, and you would not want that,
now would you, being the patrons of art that you all are,
and after all you will recognize that I have my own life
to live my own pursuit of happiness to think of while
even silverfish and cockroaches and rats and millions of
omnivorous uncivil and ununiformed creatures are
jumping up out of the sewers or gutters and swimming
for their lives in the growing cataclysm, so that perhaps
you all will excuse me now if I run along after life and
love, for the first thing God made was love though the
second thing he made was blood, although perhaps you
would not admit that, for it is at best a rude surmise
that essence really preceded being, and the third hip

59

thing that God made was the long journey that I, not to mention everybody else, is on, yes I am on the way to myself through what I hope is love or through what at least I would take for love yes I am on my way to myself through the illusions of sense through the illusions of happiness and beauty to find that innermost swinger beyond the self, if you will further pardon me for being such a walking cliché, and so, so long, so long ma, so long dad, so long doc, so long sweet sorrow. . . .

And the whole pageant and caravansary of mastuprating citizens then turned and ran off in fourteen frantic directions and dug their own graves and fell afraid into them, and I had turned the tide, I had turned the tide of human affairs on earth with my eloquence, proving once and for all how the tongue is sharper than the sword, but still there was something missing, there was still a great void in my own life, and although I had overcome all the heavy evil in the world I had yet to find sweet love for myself, and the world could still go straight to steaming hell and back again as long as I could still find that love for myself in the narrowing perspective of the world's end in which, in a parody of a parody of painting, a dumb image of an idea fled on before me through its classic perspectives, running off some Grecian urn of earth and on over the landscape of the centuries, falling through a stained glass window or two into four million modern paintings, an impressionable idol constantly affected and transformed by her changing surroundings, and still fleeing on objectively and non-objectively before all pursuers, with her skirt growing longer and longer or shorter and shorter as each century dictated, and pausing finally to straighten her seams and put spit on her seams as she came at last to today in the Rue de Vaugirard where I had not heard the music stop and had not heard the funky bird stop singing in my turning head at a turning point of that endless bookmovie that some hack had adapted from an endless parade of figures who might have been myself in a parody of my life which was itself based upon an endless sexual fantasy centered on some vague unmet figure of love with longing hair whose eyes held what I took for speechless messages, the young fanatic heart so spare in struggle, strange in flight.

Even as now I recognized myself as the chief fanatic. It was plain to see, it was myself I was deceiving. I had a small round heart, about the size of a tomato, not heart-shaped, crenelated like a sponge, breathing. The porous I. It was a white hole, a mirror, and I was looking into it, as if I could see anything in that particular hole. A porous, bottomless hole in the wall in the back of my place in the Rue de Vaugirard. It echoed, with street cries. *Vitrier!* A glazier coming, a glazier going by, his glass on his back. Perhaps his back was also made of glass. Coming back, down the street. Hawking. *Vi- tri- eh!* echoing through all those broken streets. A priest of the street, that fellow, with his plain chant, offering to repair the world, all the cracked glasses, windows, mirrors. He'd repair my mirror. *Vi-   tri   eh!*   But dimly.

Distantly. Disappearing. Gone, through the broken mirror, into that nether world, nether window in the wall. He'd repair it, give me back a new one, a new thin one, without cracks. He'd keep the cracks, take my cracks away, to the flea market where the worn world ended, goofies and gypsies picking me over. *Veee-treeee   eh*. Going still, away. I'd out after him through the dusk streets. Why always dusk in the streets? Some kind of cataracts I was getting. Or it was the streets that had their cataracts, each one hooded, with its buildings closing over, its buildings with their hoods of awnings and marquees. Here a movie marquee, with a message on it, written in lights. *Pathé*. I'd pay, dive in, hide and seek, hide and see. A woman swimming. Words printed over her as she swam. Some kind of race she was in. Or chase. With waves, boats, goggles, a Channel shore, yachts passing, people on them, tossing heads and laughing. Her body pulled out, revives, white skin glistening, pulls off goggles, swim cap, shakes out hair, smiles, waves, embraces someone near, looks into newsreel camera with arms around that someone, the eyes still looking into the eye of the camera, into my eye, then fading, the theatre lights suddenly up, all over. I had missed the feature, if there was one. Perhaps what I had seen was the feature. Everyone getting up, straggling up the aisles, with handbags, umbrellas, wives on their arms, the movie disgorging its customers into the night, all of them staggering out looking as if they were part of the picture, the part that

62

had yet to be told or shown, all disappearing into the true darkness.

But the eyes remained, in the street, the eyes of that swimmer still on me, passing on away from me in the street. I followed nowhere, down drowned boulevards, and on, once more into the still square of Saint-Sulpice, its baroque bullfrog of a church, that church of the blind organist, still open. A night mass. Inside, Tenebrae groaned in the dark, with wrath and weeping, blind rods rattling, ash on foreheads, veiled sisters walking on their knees, Christ fallen out of his stained-glass window. And in a dark pew, far off, standing—a figure I thought I recognized, yet had never seen—the face, the figure, the body of pure longing—her face hidden in a kind of a cowl, or lace mantilla. Colored leaves of light fell on her, stained light-leaves, from a high window. She felt something on her, suddenly turned her head—and looked straight into my eyes, our looks locking over a distance as immense as night itself, for an instant as long as life. In the semi-dark it was as if some strange animal had raised her head in a clearing and suddenly met the eyes of a single other in a great forest where there were no other beasts—yet in an instant the eyes had passed over me, recognizing nothing —she was not the one I'd imagined, I was only a part of the dark her eyes had passed over, I turned and passed out again into the night itself, a night not as real nor as dark as that inside.

On across the Square, on toward Saint-Germain, in the Rue de Seine, descending, I was

caught by another pair of eyes, a pair of ancient ivory
opera glasses, examining me from a closed junkshop
window, the glasses staring out at me from a heap of
rings and books and beads and fake hair and detached
plaster hands and a truss and a sandless hourglass and
a bust and a head with two faces and beheaded chess-
men and lead soldiers and an ebony baton pointing nowhere, directing nothing, and a ship stranded on a canvas river with dusty sails astray in a windless world,
and the brown hood of a monk with arms raised, the
hollow hood in darkness as if still hiding a head, the
arms reaching out as I passed out of that street and
across the Boulevard Saint-Germain to the Café Mabillon where it stood infinitely weary at a corner of another
street. Through its revolving door, I peered in, looking
for the waiter Lubin among the corduroy faces. Not tonight. His night off. Across the boulevard again, back
toward Saint-Sulpice, my shoes still moved in flight and
pursuit, I in them still. Just off that Place again, in the
corner of another street, all began again. Lights of a
dim café outlined the sitting customer. A single, squatting figure on the terrace. The waiter Lubin in a dark
overcoat, collar turned up, though it was not cold. The
waiter Lubin had the face of a great shy dog, with deep
distracted eyes, but with jutted jaw asserting his existence in the present. He saw me with those eyes, his
arm swung around and stopped me. Saucers of numer-
ous already-consumed drinks covered the small round
marble table upon which an ashtray had been upset, the
butts of little brown cigarillos scattered about.

'Listen,' Lubin said, swinging his arm about and pressing me into a chair, 'Listen, will you—I'll tell you—about your sweet wandered dollies, all right—' His jaw was meant to cup a violin, or to clench a bone, clinging to it, lifted off the earth. And the bone was his life. 'Listen, I'll tell you, if you'd only listen— What is it makes the world tack about and return posting to its home buoy, tolling the Misericordia with a clapper of cheese? Sweet Jesus, hear my song, take care of all swimming beasts!'

I'd seen this face of his in somebody else's painting. No, that was not it, exactly. He was, rather, a bent character out of those Twenties books, one of those American-in-Paris books, still hanging on to haunt another generation, ensnaring me in his moldy old preoccupations. Maybe he'd even been away for a decade or two or three, only this year returned to his old haunts, expecting to find the same American characters in their old places, the old plot to continue where he had left off. Well, I did not fit in, do what he could with his illusions, just like these too familiar streets and this Square loaded with decades and centuries and generations of bathetic associations poured out of every famous postcard painting and book, every street-name dripping with gummy references to somebody else's famous past, and each generation of cast-up foreigners wandering stupid through the same hackneyed scenes, each one a hung-up walking cliché, and corny as the scene was it continued to repeat itself, over and over, every decade, and new battalions and bottomless boatloads of the same types arriving annually forever. And there I sat as if a part of it, as if I couldn't escape it either, whereas all I really had to do was get up and haunt some other, distant part of town where the stones were not so worn down. I did not get up. Lubin had my arm. He signaled the waiter inside, holding up two spread fingers.

'Listen, I'm as old as a forgotten orgasm but does that make any difference to anyone? Has the fished-up heart changed any? Has Aphrodite grown a beard, or night become a Dobbs Ferry virgin? Not so easy, not so easy as all that.' He was a cliché of a character come back to the scene of his former book, only somehow now I had crept into the old plot, somehow now I became the new victim of it. He spoke English with an American accent, had been in the States a long time but, when he was drinking, his Viennese origins crept back into his voice. He drank off half of his new drink, pushed the other toward me. 'Here you come.' He had my arm, shaking it. 'Here you come, digging up the past for me with your hunting eyes. Who fished you up, anyway, who fished the murex up?' Somewhere a toilet flushed. Fishface, I drank the Ricard that looked like green fog in the glass.

'Is it,' he had my shoulder again, 'is it my own past swimming up before me, or isn't it? An American like you with a label like Raffine! Dung of Europa, aren't we the lost tribesmen, and me your wandered father come back again? The same wash, in a different bundle, sent to be laun-

66

dered in America. The long return!' He belched loudly, the sweet, sticky taste of Ricard on his breath. I drank. He had hold of my knee, rocking back and forth. 'Born by inadvertence, Master Raffine, you pulled up your drawers and came out, only to find yourself in another country, wandering around lost between nowhere and here, neither fish nor whore, with no holy water stoup to call your own—*Garçon!*' He belched and waved, pulled out a large torn handkerchief and mopped his face, opened his coat, fanning himself, while the waiter came and went, leaving two more green drinks. Lubin drank, silent, as if he had forgotten me. Pigeons whirred in the Square beyond the corner, settled and walked around under the trees.

'Allow me to introduce myself.' He swept his arm in a small bow in my direction. 'The bilious tag-end of your future, belching and hollering for one more drink—' He fell silent, distracted again. I drank, I wanted to get up, I wanted to go out among the pigeons and lie on the grass. I had forgotten there was no grass in the Square. I had lived this before, and in the former scene there had been grass. I still wanted to get up. It wasn't the grass, then, that made me want to get up. He had my arm. Somewhere a toilet flushed.

'For Christ's sweet sake,' he began again, 'wait for me! Asking me where *she* lives! As if you could call it that, as if it could make any difference to you beside which stranger she was sleeping. Well, I'll explain her to you all right, Little Miss Misery, the calamity kid, let me tell you—waiters and whores like night editors of a scandal sheet, digesting everybody's entrails. Only this time it's my own. The hand that grips the genitals, love plays the deep-sea catch—' He drank. 'Haunting the cafés to find her! Ah, where gone? Do you think, all this mothering time, she's been hiding downstairs in the WC, that noble signpost of British colonialism?' I drank. He looked into the dark square as if searching a mislaid clue to his life. A clue or a clou or a clef. A key. He raised his eyebrows, as if he had almost caught sight of what he looked for, across the square. 'Ah yes, of course, twice her age, yes. However—back then—' His eye in the sky, it fixed upon the black round towers of the church. Huge, ponderous, they hung in the night, sledge hammers poised. He spoke on, intently. 'Twice her age, was I—what decade is it, who can tell? Only I see myself in the revolving door, an earlier Andy Raffine on the prowl for the woman I had never met or made—on and on—and all found out at last in their true turned flesh, poor grounded angels—a delicate point of horror—' His voice a bad stage whisper, he was a ham actor regurgitating a well-known drama in another language, a curiously Greek drama through which I had sat before yet could not remember the end, for the characters had been changed about, the dialogue changed to suit, and Greek tragedy was blind, a lover kills his lover, thinking her the twin. 'Garçon.' He did not raise his voice, his eye still in the sky. I raised two spread fingers. The Ricard sang, a liberated toad in my hand, the night went round, a black carrousel, a revolving stage. His eyes

68

came back, his arm on mine again, tugging at it, his face up close.

'My wife, do you understand, now, at last? My wife, so-called, and no one bothering to deny it. And do you imagine, if I were your age it would make any difference? Do you imagine it would do any good, do you—' He left it hanging, stared off again. I had never seen her in white daylight, had only glimpsed her in the night streets, her head half-hidden. The play was over already, while I sat still listening for the next line, expecting myself to walk on the stage at any moment, have something to say about it, take a hand in the action, the belated fish-eyed protagonist arriving too late on the scene, somehow still a part of it.

'Do you suppose,' he spoke on, as if he had not been silent, 'that I don't know what's been going on, for years, who knows how long? From the beginning—ah, of course, there was a beginning—back when she was still doing her statues— ah yes, those statues—' He laughed a kind of a snort. 'And that studio—ah yes, I had forgotten—her studio! How long since she had that studio—she has no studio, my sainted friend, do you understand—and those statues —yes, you guessed it—all herself—all as she imagined her poor sweet self—as she was—as she actually was?' It was almost a question. 'Who knows? I knew—sure, that was it—I saw her in her statues too, when she was doing them back then—but even then—who knows when she started, when it started? I know. When she taught sculpture to the blind, at the Ecole Nationale des Aveu-

69

gles, back before I became *garçon*. Teaching the blind!'
He snorted again. 'They taught *her*, in the dark. In the
blind we see ourselves, they make us recognize ourselves, seeing ourselves for the first time. They have the
advantage of simplification, living by each other's
voices, without the necessity of interpreting the look in
the eye, like lovers always telephoning, or radio people
not required to act their words—I went to their rooms,
with her, once, for a party. And there they all were
dancing and singing, laughing and walking around. It
was only after I fell over a sofa full of lovers that they
realized they had forgotten to turn on the lights. It was
a normal situation—who carries crutches who has no use
for them? They see night as day, and the night they
know for what it may be—' The night turned round, a
phono revolving, a black disc, repeating itself, a black
parrot in a cage with a needle beak. It spoke on. 'The
blind lovers on the couch I tripped over had a public
privacy which I interrupted with the seeing-eye, vul-
garizing a closed world. It was the Well of the Saints
all over again—two people ugly to the eye, knowing
each other beautiful— Only when the light was restored,
I was the only sufferer.'

It was not a record going around,
it was a far accordion man, down the street, by a de-
funct Metro entrance, a shapeless figure, squeezing his
mushy box. Lubin swayed in his seat to the music,
flapped his arms, mimicking the accordionist, crooned
loudly in burlesque imitation, '*M'sieur Le Noble est
très triste, depuis sa femme l'a quitté— M'sieur Le*
70

Noble se mouche—' His voice cracked on *mouche,* and he coughed, his flapped arms falling, a bird of prey come to roost. 'The only sufferer!' he shouted. 'According to whom? Only when the light was restored, finally, I saw her for the first time—'

The music again, without words, the black disc still revolving, the cornball story continued, all came back, the hole I had imagined, the studio I had imagined, next door, through the hole that had been real, the parrot turning twice about. I had seen the statues in that gallery, they had been real. He said he had seen her, on a couch, in the next room, when the light was restored, the candles, the record going round, her form on the couch, wind at the window, curtains blown in, two candles guttering, darkness, over and over, and lights again, finally, the statues falling, one by one, dismembered, a blind someone kissing her hair, her throat, the hollows of her throat, her breasts, moaning, mouth on mouth. I had not heard the music stop. Silence stretched itself, somewhere a toilet flushed. Or a loud bidet. A cold white river ran away.

Lubin had pulled himself up, looked smaller somehow. When he spoke, his voice came out small. 'Should I say I was expecting you, or merely that I knew you would arrive? She was here tonight, if you want to know, sitting here as quiet as any calamity, until she saw another "long-lost friend" go by—then off, after him, without paying, before I could say *merde, alors* or *Hail, Caesar—'* He seemed now to see me for the first time, having just discovered me sitting there. 'So, it's you is it? And when the child is to be weaned, the mother blackens her breast, blackens her—a blind tragedian misleading the blind, I've blackened hers for you—but don't sit there like some tit-willow dowager who has entered a brothel by mistake. Do not hurry yourself. This is not the death of the famous freighted heart. Do not trouble yourself. You'll find your long-lost where you'd always known she lay, spread-eagled in the night, waiting, with the hot iron of love. Stick around! There's still a little time for counting the saucers. The love in the closet will keep, the clothes will fit another student—' Silence. A toilet flushed. Or a bidet.

'Do you,' Lubin said after a long while, 'do you ever go into the churches, do you ever get taken with going into any church you happen to come upon, no matter whose or where—the impulse to kneel as irresistible as any other Mother Nature's call, one private place or *pissoir* as useful as another?' The waiter was coming, putting the wicker chairs up on the tables. The night had not stopped turning, the ferris wheel still went round after the music stopped, still turning with its empty seats and riderless horses. The waiter was putting the horses up on the round tables, setting them upside down, their straw legs in the air, pawing. Lubin held to the table, swaying, leaning forward like a rider. I rose, and he still had my arm.

'Stick around, will you! Not so fast, will you! You'll still get there in plenty of time, she'll still be waiting—' The

72

waiter was clearing our table, marking down the saucers in his little book. 'On me,' Lubin told him, making a small courtly gesture with his free hand, the other still holding me. 'All on me—Patron—' He tucked the hand in his vest. 'Patron of strangers, friend to crossbreeds, and—' He rose halfway, swayed considerably, but maintained his stance. 'Sponsor of all legal and blessed coition—though I am no *schatchen,* pardon me—' He belched and swung his free arm in the grand gesture, but immediately retracted it. 'I merely wish to state that the lady is at present returned, that she is, as they say in the stage directions, "within." I should say Please Do Not Disturb. Quiet, as the Pullman Company reminds us, is requested for the benefit of those who have re— Oh, but I wish she had, and there's the blear spot that will not rub—' The hand holding me slipped and fell, Lubin fell back in his chair, his voice fell with him. 'Oh the stone angels we run after, each of us after his own, and the heart an involuntary muscle after all, as here you come again, down the same alley— Twice by inadvertence, once by design, he challenges his destiny—it comes when he—oh for the love of dangling Christ, do I have to spell it all out for you, does the night editor have to run the Lost and Found column too!' The ground continued to go round, tilting. I grasped the turning table, as Lubin began to shout, half to himself. 'Oh, for the love of dangling—sure she's here all right— right upstairs, if you have to know—my hotel, or I should say "our" hotel—yes, go right on, right up, right upstairs, right—' The entrance was there, just to the right of the café awning, with its dim smoked bulb over it, like the burning end of a cigarette. Or like the dim gleam of a merrygoround ring which I, leaning out, might still reach for. I was on the edge of the whirling platform of the terrace, it at last stopped turning, Lubin shouting at me, flapping his arms, 'Yes! That's it—tell her I sent you—by all means—we'll not mention the fee —tell her you already—'

II

I had lost and was searching for something on the stones
of the Square, in an hour I no longer recognized, the
performance over, the characters gone through their
last exit, I an extra who returned to find something he'd
dropped on the boards, or in a dressingroom. Or I was
merely one of the audience who could not go home
without finding what he had lost, a key dropped under
a seat, or at a stage-door where a dim light still burned.
Now the shuttered Square was suddenly alive with a
whirring of wings, in the loud end of dark, beating
about my head. Something had aroused the pigeons,

and they arose from the black pavement, from corniced ledges, deserted benches, into the hushed, dry air, circling about me, with strange beaked cries. As suddenly they settled again, stones thrown to earth, flesh stones fallen, finally wingless. They walked about now, drunkenly, brooding to themselves on the stones of the Square, like castaway sailors waded ashore, cocking heads and eyes at the ground and the sky as if searching for something all had lost. It was a search for a lost community, and one's true *pays natal* was said to be the place in which one experienced one's first deep emotion, but there was a native birthplace, a native country, far before that. And the womb all fell out of was merely the last location of that community, was only the last site of it, the last station on the line that ran from that far country, the last waitingroom or *salle des pas perdus* in which love met blood. Still both had met in us, we were its last synthesis, its latest conjunction, we fell out into the world with that community still in us, if it were anywhere still it could be no other place, within the sites of ourselves, hidden, unsee-able, as the eye cannot see itself, love dissolved, invisible, lost in our blood, not lost, yet not here. Not here, in the spent dark. Yet I made no progress away. My feet moved away, pavement slipped under, I advanced nowhere, stationary, running. I returned and returned through the stone gallery of the Square that led back and back to the door with its cigarette light in its blind mouth, opening and closing.

Dawn pointed, over the church of Saint-Sulpice. Its towers

76

moved upward in the first light, hung over me. In the high forgotten sky, light bred, echoed, outlining rooftops, chimneypots, earth revolving away. On that treadmill of earth which was the site of myself, my feet moved, and I did not, I was a vacated site, a vacant spot detached, as darkness still tossed up bits of wreckage, cornerstones, bottles, lampposts adrift, broken shutters, blown posters, scraps of paper whirled and tossed, tossed and whirled in the dawn wind. I was an extra who had mislaid something important to him alone while performing a walk-on part anyone could perform, and now the only witnesses that remained were the statues of four famous dead preachers around the still fountains in the center of the Square, and they had no answer, they stared out, finally wordless, not meant to be confronted at this hour. A bird, a shadow, a dark wind blew across the shaken sky, and a wind came up like a gale of tongues, sweeping up a sleeping cat, an empty ashcan, a distant man. Paper sky now. A streetlight burnt in it. Paper lily. Streetsweepers coming, swept me before them. Distant dogs gave off a faint, excessive desolation, rooks cawed and called, called and cawed, with dark flash, flutter of wing. What phono birds were they? They cried into an existence that still represented itself as one long shifting sequence of events and searches, an existence that still popped up perpetually out of that flat landscape, issuing forth from every perspective of streets, avenues, and Metro entrances, a sequence through which I moved hardly somnambulant, making no progress out of my bag of flesh.

A soiled piece of string still held it tied together, I still could not untie it, to find the skinless frank beneath. Still the wind that blew in breathing gusts along the Rue de Seine might blow me out of my skin. I went before it, down to the Seine. There the air and the trees fell still, though butterflies still blew about, paper whimsies, crepe birds. Lost petals, blown along the quais, toward Saint-Michel, on past it. Candy day coming, all waked, busses began, the Metros stirred their iron snakes. I'd climb on one, for a single Metro ticket I'd ride out of it, free, into the open country. Or beyond. I'd take a Metro to another country, anywhere, away, if I could find a subway entrance in the ground, in the asphalt of the city that poured out before me as if some great megalopolitan cement truck with whirling mixer moved along before me manufacturing existence, pouring out the streets and houses, boulevards and sidewalks, in a single continuous operation, and the sidewalk unwinding as if squeezed from a tube, an endless ribbon of asphalt upon which sprang to life myriad faces figures autos babies baby-carriages automats and signs, the moving carpet of it slipping back under my feet.

In the Square of Julien-le-Pauvre, children were already playing, imitating marching soldiers and battles, twittering and shrieking like swallows, and along the bent paths of the little park a cat stalked a bird, a child in frills stalked the cat, a nurse in frills with a bird's nest hat stalked the child, and she had had other professions, her pink lace petticoat over black stockings, her profoundly gaudy

78

smile turned on me, while from her throat came a gaudy cackle, her lips without gums giving off an obscene sucking echo of herself at an earlier age in heat of night clutching lover to groin. I saw now I had found some kind of key, I had picked it up *back there*, without knowing. It was a key I could insert into every woman, or into every human, or into every animal, and once inserted it would turn the soul of things as they were, or as they might very well be. It was a new painting-knife with which to scrape things down to the bare bones and leaded ground. I would go away on a long trip and scrape the world down with it. With the last of my mother's money, with the last of mother, I'd get out of my skin, turning the key as I went. To begin with this particular woman before me, as an example, she had camembert skin, coitus but a spasm in her memory, yet still she wore some old faded flower at her throat, or rather at her breast, as if she still had the figure for it, *sa gorge mûre bombant sous un tricot rose,* forty years before, on the prowl for *her* community. The breasts fell, the poppies fell with them, still she hunted, now by the decayed façade of Saint-Julien-le-Pauvre's damp church in which the stone face of the Virgin was streaked with a green leprosy, her lips with stone gums giving off a lonely sucking sound, an old dame in end of night, clutching pillow to groin, still waiting for her Noel, and this stone figure an artist's representation of that Community, although if a priest were to come by and ask why I was not weeping, I would have to say 'I am not of the parish.' Leaves drifted by like fish, and like a waker between dreams, I was walking away from that parish, through the bent stereopticon streets.

Here a door was my Metro entrance, a blind man by it, with a cardboard box around his neck. Called me as I passed. His hand in the shape of a claw made a sign of the zodiac, a sign meant for me, a scorpio, a finger crooked at me, he cocked his head at me, gave me a whistle. He sang some sort of palinode under his breath. Not a song but a whisper, a salespitch. . . . *Neckties . . . Shoelaces.* . . . Over and over. Crooking his crabby finger at me all the while, cocking his head. As if to say I Want You. *You.* Over and over, the crooked finger, the cocked eye, the low whistle, the pitch. *Neckties. . . . Razorblades.* Hopeless, intoning. I was rooted, a tree in the pavement by the entrance, incapable of ever taking the Metro, or of moving at all. The finger crooked, the head cocked, and from time to time he stroked the sides of his nose with the edge of a hand that appeared dead, the fingers oddly stiff and distended. He grew younger, fatter, as I watched, became myself, standing there with a sudden shower of rain running down my face and off my chin into the shoebox, and I felt the wet box and I fingered the wet laces in the box all tangled together like string, knotted together, end on end. A noose of string-like neckties stretched around my neck, supporting the box, and the box gave off a faint, woody perfume, as of hair. The laces were tangled hair among which small bottles of scent had broken. I tasted the rain running down my face and recognized the perfume that smelled of woman's hair, and it ran down into the corners of my eyes. My eyes twisted with women's hairpins in them, I looked out with buttonhook vision, then with no vision at all, and I was the blind man, and I threw the box off and plunged down into the station, looking for any train, pulled up by a cool fountain, drank. No, it was not a fountain. It tasted of shadows, a man melted in a cup of cinders. Heavy water, in a stoup. The Metro station was of a gothic design. *Please don't drink the holy water* said a sign. Odor of incense and rose leaves. But prayer, being pure, could not smell, even of incense. No, I was wrong about that, it was not a fountain in a church, it was really the underground vault of the Metro as I'd first supposed, with a drinking fountain shaped like a stoup, with the sticky-sweet sound of an accordion man sitting on stumps on the platform, and the morning rush-hour crowd coming. A man with a bullfish face took my ticket, and I was swept up in the surge of a horde of animals rushing along the platforms and throwing themselves into long oblong boxes on wheels, and I was swept into one of those coffins which immediately went wheeling off into a black tunnel, a nightmaze metroland in which were twenty-four hours of night in a day. It was a black boat I was on, rocking onward. Bustards beat about the sides of it. It was a whole string of rowboats I was in, rocking onward through a tunnel of love on an underground Seine or Styx. The torches of lights leaned out over, the rowboats knocked together, end to end, in the river. No, not a river. A flood. The human museum of the Metro was flooded, and I remembered the keeper had been a bull-fish, and he was up in the cab ahead now, wearing a ferryboat captain's hat, ferrying us all over his underground river, and now there was a hole of light and a kind of a dock, and all piled out, running, swimming, climbing over each other, pawing each other. It was some kind of transfer point at the end of the shuttle, a Times Square turning point, and some of the animals succeeded in climbing up and out through holes of earth where the sky itself had opened up, lit with lightning, thunder ricocheting off the earth, and a lake had fallen into the Place Montparnasse through which clothed figures swam to floating arks of busses. But part of the earth opened up right in front of the Gare Montparnasse and swallowed everybody again, closing up like a big bite and leaving odds and ends of bodies and coattails and neckties sticking out, and I was running in socks of chewing gum through another underground tunnel into the Gare Montparnasse and through its *salle des pas perdus* and out towards its platforms where the subway had turned into one last long train. It puffed and hooted, impatient to be off through the same rain that was still falling, and at the entrance to the first dark coach was the same blind man, or another blind man with the same cardboard box, or another cardboard box with the same laces in it, or other white laces of string with the same knots, and the man intoning the same old refrain of *razorblades neckties string,* and the string wound around my neck and knotted around my throat and supported my box of broken perfume that dripped

82

down everywhere, soaking me. Only the man who was myself now wore a conductor's cap with a certain number on it in Roman lettering, and I jumped into the subway that had turned into a real train just as with a great puff and grunt it broke loose and started tearing down its restless jumping terrestrial track.

Myself to find my witless self anew on the old Orient Express out of myself which was not going to the Orient although its ringing bell sounded like the sound of three hands clapping through every tunnel where Buddha sat silently turning on and off the flashing signal lights of his enigmatic smile and tripping hidden switches which always succeeded in keeping the train of my thought from going right through him where he sat in the full lotus position, while in every other tunnel the original Creator, himself an agnostic, wore another of the masks of his various incarnations and blinked on and off *his* signal lights to the train which, like some eternally triumphant penis, went bursting on through every tunnel and obstruction regardless of the stop-and-go signals, but in the eternal crawling night of the tunnels there was no destination, there was only the darkness that made all stand still, as if there were really nowhere to go, and Buddha nodding that this was the case exactly, though I still smelled the faint woody smell of woman that had seeped in everywhere in the train, but it was growing fainter and fainter all the time, and from the back observation platform I could see the world receding, could see Paris receding at the shrinking hole at the end of a tunnel, a

83

tattered arras, a far, dim fabric, an intricate image of a half-life I led and which I now thought to leave behind by running away from it through the length of the train, through crowded compartments and corridors, tripping over bodies and legs, while as the train curved out of another tunnel and into daylight I could see signs on the sides of the cars ahead reading GENEVE-MILANO-ISTANBUL, but the car I was in was not going to Istanbul although I could not see what its sign read, rocking on through lighted landscapes of flooded fields and battlements to high snow mountains and on and on rocking and blowing through a high country where small stations flew by like stone birds, and it was all the trains I had ever ridden on, hitched together with universal couplings, all the rods I had ever ridden now slithering together into one long track over myriad crazy roadbeds of desire, and all the travelers that had ever traveled merged in myself, speaking sixty-six languages, with all the languages dubbed together into one great supranational soundtrack with multilingual simultaneous translation, a long-playing record of talking existence. It was a runaway train moving trackless over infusorial earth, and everywhere in the world trains and travelers rushing somewhere, hurtling horizontal in bedwagons or hanging onto swinging subway straps, each one of them a perambulant palimpsest, his flesh containing all his memories, each his own *porteur*, carrying everything he'd been, each a waitingroom full of trunks and lovers, jockstraps and friends, suitcases and wives, brothers and sis-

84

ters and baby carriages, skirts and trousers and sisters and mothers and fathers and sons.

But the Customs men were coming to put a stop to it, the Customs men were going to prevent these foreign illusions from crossing their borders, the Swiss Customs men were coming through the train looking at everybody's passports and papers, shaking their heads this way and that over them, considering the osmosis of cultures in a land that allowed no illusions, and one of the inspectors at the Swiss border had a nervous tic and kept shaking his head to himself all the time as if continually puzzled, but when he got up to where I was he stopped twitching and said 'Razorblades? Shoelaces?' Rain dripped down suddenly from his cap, and the number on his cap was the same as my age, and with a great burst of disquieting laughter he started shaking me, frisking me, shouting, 'Haven't you anything at all to declare? Where've you hidden your earth's baggage? Nothing of your own to declare! Don't you even have a hat and a tie?' 'Well, yes,' I said, 'come to think of it, I have got something to declare—' And mounting the back of a seat and tucking my hand in my vest, I declaimed to the inhabitants of the car as follows: 'Yes, indeed, I have something of my own to declare, and I'll seize the fat-boy's day and declare it, for my ass is out and I'm bare, my heart is bare-ass bare, if you can bear it, and I'm wide open, although I climb no cool mountains, write no sawmill haikus, for Pilot Palinurus, too fat to climb, too fat to swim, fell into the sea and was free, yes, Pilot Palinurus sailed away

85

from his lost youth, remorse and folly, though still hung-up on some pale siren, lost in the Zambesi of her smile, and her blue breasts are over my shoulder as I come floating by, as I arrive in a shambles of childbirth to claim my flippy home in the unconscious, and someone all this time combing the earth with a pocketcomb, and with a touch of Piblokto madness I come falling down through your still ice-caps in Switzer's Land in a lack-love sickness for some unmet androgynous angel, so wing me no dingbats for I'll find my way, a pegamoid sloth who falling and falling through your high land will finally reach the dead sea level of things, the dead level where all that grows can grow only upward, and the Dead Sea not one of Jesu's favorite places, for the hair on his brow was low and still grew down, and the hair of my low brow still over my eyes and no place to part it, half-a-Jew onward, a wandered one who never saw the sin-side, inside of a synagogue, and so fell down, swung down, a swingy jew's harp in a tree, and so fall down to the far and fishy subterranean mediterranean meditating sea that laps your adriantic shore where I'll yet float in the tin of my boat, my sardine boat, a jew-down at sunset, a fart of a fish preserved in the salt of my fat, my sardine can alack, the tongue for a Viking sail, your fishy fellow found at last a drag upon the earth who yet would climb, and the clock of the sea still to be stopped if I am not to fall forever through its face, through the salt reality that stops all, my pimpled face turned to a sea-green leprosy to eat at last the blackbook of mind, and my mouth too large to breathe through the eye of a needle, though the fat skin breathes and I sweat too much, so farewell philosophy, farewell youth, farewell France, where in a piece of string I found myself, the one and only girl-in-white curled up, inside of me, and the white oedipus eye of the Alps revolving, staring down on the all of it, and the map of Paris burned upon my brainpan, for there can be complete lists of one's loving, there can be complete lists of my loving, with memories of almost-love the squirm-roots of heaven, and I can still declare that in a sea of a dig of a way I know no other glib of living to be done, know no breathing but the turning tide of it, and even if eating bananas increases sexual potency there is still a still of love, a reservoir of it that never changes its level in the dead sea of things, a constant quantity of love that remains forever in the earth, even though in dry seasons it evaporate and be drawn up into air, it still floats there, ready to descend again in the first sperm rain, and so goes round with us in our fifteen miles of atmosphere, and I one of those pigeons or seagulls blowing South over the linen landscape, a high gull over a gothic landscape that melts into the stones of Venice, a black iron bird rocketing through snow and blowing a monster whistle and belching smoke, a frenzy bird that flies above and beyond and behind a psychopathology of hysteria, an artist's talking parrot paring its fingernails, a goony bird in the Black Forest contemplating Kierkegaard and God, and have you been back to any forest lately, have you been back to your own forest, have you of late revisited the dark trees? as we flit past your life of stations and

87

women where Death waves a lantern at every country crossroad and your eternal tongue and teeth fall out in greeting? He's holding a light, Look, Look, he cries, *Yours! Yours!* And through another tunnel the light plunges, out. Never worry, you'll never refind it, gone, gone. Father climb over wooden chairs, Annalivia's coming home, but her teeth are out, her brassiere's backwards, a sea-change made among the Greek *hetaerae*, a piece of string to give the Custom man, the salt collector with the sardine tongue, and as for me let me finally declare as he comes that I have only the original Mona Lisa with me to be declared, a thing of small worth and smaller concern, I assure you, and not half as valuable as Van Gogh's ear which various subversive artists still have concealed in their paintboxes, if you will but search them, but as I was saying this here Mona Lisa is no more than the expression of a moaning leisure or satiety resulting from that eternal dame having just eaten her husband, note the famous enigmatic smile of containment if not of contentment, see how you can almost see a hair of his beard still sticking out of a corner of her mouth, like the tiny tail of a swallowed goldfish, and I want therefore to declare that as in the end life imitates art and that as the flushing of bidets signaled the end of an era, so the final burying of my moaning Lizzie along with Googie's ear shall bring about finally the long overdue millennium of art and life, the first and final real meeting of the two, each seeing the other bare for the first time, for there is no Orphic explanation of the world and no anthropomorphic and no analogic and no mystic explanation and no historic and no hysteric explanation and no ethnological mythological geological anthropological geopolitical metaphysical religio-medical audio-visual antedeluvial prehistorical mephistophical philosophical psychological psychosomatical circumstantial epigrammatical aphoristical linguistical semantical psychical apocryphal phenomenal explanation, and, even though organized society in the form of governments may be evil in itself, pockets of anarchism are still generated in the savage, formless movement of life, and the rebel will always reject divinity, for it would be a strange form of love indeed in which rebellion did not exist, and the true rebel hero, drag that he is, will always set forth to reconquer what he already owns, for the values of life are constantly and perpetually to be re-deduced from the conditions of living, the sense of human motivation most profound in what is most profoundly of the present, and the subject of life is not death, and he who paints another Mona Lisa smile is still perpetuating outdated information, and pocket-combs will yet win and poets sitting on mountain-tips call each other on golden telephones, and Yogurt win though toothbrushes die, and dogs do it while cats wail, and a wiggy God win out though not in his sundaysuit, and Barkus still willing while Falsies fall and tits triumph, and the living newspaper of humanity thrown anew on the porch each morning will win, Dick Tracy die with his hoods and Mingus win with Felonious Monk, GoodforyouGuinness will win, Canarsie's angels will win, Woolworth canaries will win, the Yellow Pages will win, and under den Linden trees in Boston Common all cops die as blonds roll over and sing in the Fall leaves, and backyard dawns over the American continent hold their own while tickertape fails and falls, for the mad seeing-eye dog of the fourth person singular is coming, the cool eye of the fourth person singular of which nobody speaks is coming to single out and separate the light from illusion in all mascara nights as a Jean Valjean comes drunken swimming up out of underground Metros, a fatso Caruso singing lost in the tunnels, a Yonkers Villon with hair in his eyes swimming up through the flooded subway exits and so goes seeing new all up and down world's street, with prying painter's eye but nothing to see but himself, in streetsigns, churches, breasts and arms and faces, lightswitches, windows, erasers and coffeepots, moons and trees and *trucs* and pairs of illusive glasses and pairs of pants and sandwichmen and women popping out of automats and the third tree of reflected vision and nothing to find but self and a great wind blowing through all my painting but no more *tremping* of *gâteaux* no more the sound of axes in the wood the voiceless vision the soundless soughless bells and the whole calamitous enunciation the dog beneath the skinless frank of things re-seen in the day of the night of existence but a lantern-jawed camera obscure sprouting signals to corrode away any adjective skin or carapace in a rapt euphoria of time in space in which Robbe-Grillet meets Robespierre and has a final vision of the pathetic fallacy of the earth's sadness and the unmystery of things unhidden in a certain number of sites and people hidden in their selfmade beds and in their own bathetic fallacies and in their hideouts of street-directories phone books and train schedules and no more painted novels of epiphanies no more watercolor paintings of the Easter Egg but signals in the unfaced thing and face where nothing avails in the thoughtless escape the unwigged woman running through the fields of wheat and blowing branches where the earth moves and moving loves, and so at last uncovers, and so at last is uncovered what really's going on, what goes, what shakes, what's really shaking in the world, as I go walking down sadsackville's street and out the drafty corridor at its very end where all begins anew on a new *table-rase* of cleansed perception and I am a child again a bounce baby a bullyboy who hears Don't spill Don't put your elbows on the table and yesterday I burnt my doghouse and mommy said It's bad mommy said Go to your room mommy said I was bad and I am a big boy and mommy is a red table and I made my dog an ear I used my crayolas and my scissors I pasted my dog's ear on his head I used a hammer to tack it a hammer daddy for I had no daddy-o I had no foreman on the job to help erect my tinkertoy erector-set and so went walking so go walking on through that longest town where cries the mad blind owl with eyes a question of ontology to answer which the staring owl must blink and blink upon me where I walked and walk still wearing rubber sandals and sad socks of chewing gum and throwing old chimeras over my shoulder where the go-go signals still turn on and off and broken bells

spill out their scoopings from the still of sound and
every cool creeper of midnights seeking his morning
and the twenty-six horses of his apprenticeship pulling
him along over the roadbed cobbles where the wordless
woman in the tight skirt still drops seeds of delirium behind her in the street as she fleeting still disappears perpetually like a true hung-up descendant of all pale idols
who dance and bound to death among skyscrapers and
the iron trams clanging forever into death and darkness
in the iron dusk in the end of the Queen's Road and this
all illusion again for I have slipped off again, pardon
me, slipped off the true new Big Table of perception on
which the soulbridge between all things of earth and
man has been abolished so that objects are no longer
the peaceful and domesticated objects that look back at
man and reflect himself like so many mirrors, no longer
objects that in every association reflect sentiments man
has imparted to them, as for instance the moon with a
man in it made of cheese, or as for instance the moon
made of lovers, or as for instance the moon in June supposed to be a lover's lantern or as for instance a chest-
nut tree root in a public garden black with man-made
associations of eternal growing rooting pushing human
life or by association becoming a black fingernail or a
snake or a fat foot or a vulture's claw or some other
thing it is not and the world of things thus thoroughly
contaminated or enriched, depending how you look at
it, by man's emotions, and all made into mirrors of himself and his feelings as if this Mont Blanc now before
me has been waiting for me here in the 'heart' of the

Alps since prehistoric times, standing there loaded with ideas of enduring greatness and purity in the old humanism of predestination as if the whole unvarying universe and I had but a single soul and a single secret and thus falsely all life seen as predestined in a false identity with Nature, a bond between man's spirit and all things and the world of things falsely become the depository of all aspirations toward immortality, but I keep slipping off the new wiped-off table because I and no one has the true fourth sight to see without the old associational turning eye that turns all it sees into its own, and it is this fourth person singular voice of which nobody speaks but which still exists unvoiced that will speak in the eye of tomorrow's seeing man and which will see truly how there is no rapport of any kind between himself and natural objects except a rapport of strangeness, and the rapport between man and nature a sympathetic illusion eternally perpetuated by man made into painters and poets and a rose is a rose is not a bleeding heart and the great soul-bridge is down the great soul-bridge between a man and a rose or a man and a church steeple or man and a magic mountain is down the bridge blown up at last in every dreaming artist's face as still our drag of a mythological hero undertakes many labors and must still forge his own destiny and is always abducted by his parents from the stateless reservoir of unborn unarticulated hungry humanity and is snatched by the father out of that reservoir and thrown headlong into the waiting carryall of the mother who rolls off through the 'birthing' night into the 'waking'

world where at last she uncovers the puling infantine
He and thrusts him forward with scissorleg motion into
the first day and her blue breasts are over his shoulder
and this mythological hero who is always myself is
always abducted from his parents and spirited away at
age One and left upon seven hills and doorsteps subway platforms rafts and drifting ships where like a far
note in a blue bottle he is left to toss upon the sea to
unknown lands or lakes and cast upon cloudy shores
trailing clouds of unglory as he comes and the hero who
is always myself aspires to the absolute for already he
is caged in it and trapped in Mont Blanc's white absolute fallacy and he wants to do everything and see
everything and taste smell feel fuck everything to half-
ass forge in the recapitulated ontogeny of the smith-
sonian smithie of his sole consciousness that fourth person singular who is the true final swinger engaged in
the final pure digging of everything and everyone and
so half-awakening to that first awareness of what it is
To Dig he finds himself in his own body in an orphan's
home cast-up in an orphanage to end all orphanages
where in swaddled clothes he eats the undercooked
tapioca cats-eyes of baby reality and pukes his way into
someone's heart who takes him away and away he goes
and the next thing he knows he is walking and he is
walking away from it all and he is walking through
those nightwood streets of his own in the youth of that
year and in the youth of that life which he has already
just begun to recover and which is already irrecover-
able in the woolly womb he's already lost and found and

lost again and the hero not searching in spite of all prop-
aganda to the contrary the hero not searching for something like his father mother sister brother who will always and forever be only ghosts by the wind ungrieved
and the hero is not looking for them and he is looking
for himself instead as he goes walking on and there he is
in another country or in side streets of hoboken canarsie new orleans chicago memphis tuscaloosa tokyo paris
and in none of these places does he find old dad the
father nor would he recognize him if he found him for
he is not looking for him for he is looking for that mirror
which is the fourth reflection of himself and which is
the final reflected unsatorical satirical vision of the
oneness of all and the final composite city of himself
seen from fourteen angles and fiftythree philosophies
and stirred into the light of a single image reflected in a
shaving mirror cracked and hanging below a single
white lightbulb in a skylighted shamble from which he
walks out wiggy into picadilly circuses of the turning
earth and around and around its columbus circles and
rond points and washington merrygorounds in autumn
capitals of the world their avenues of leaves ablaze and
he the perpetual passenger of those streets with their
continuous windows reflecting himself and possessing
him like the long continuous mirrors above the moving
windows of Simplon Expresses reflecting and possessing
the stuck ticket tokens of each passenger as well as his
hat umbrella briefcase knapsack suitcase wife as well as
the rest of the passengers with their upsidedown mus-
taches breasts lips smoking and talking and here we go

each up his own mountain with its cuckoo clock at the
top and me with my Alpenstock my Latin Quarter hat
looking like a beat boulevardier disguised as Samuel
Beckett or some other nude unnamable who got no real
cool clothes and got no real cool sportscar and got no
Go-T and cool hat and things like that and is defined as
a person who got no relatives and friends and don't have
no good stable occupation and does the opposite of
what is popular and acts very strange in society and
lives with reinforced concrete music and pad parties
and gets money from oo knows whar and lives in an
apart-ment without real furniture and wears wild beards
and tries to live in the future while the present is going
on which is how the true hung-up free cat is de-scribed
in the press where all is pressed and the true beat paint-
poet being he whose name is maude that is to say mud
that is to say muddie that is to say maudit and who lay
me on the road to H which is the first dead letter of
Heaven and Hell and all upsidedown in the mirror like
I'm climbing but where and I got the freedom of being
free from gud god I got the freedom of my pants and I'm
not involved in society although I'm involved in my own
ego and I may be masturbating when I paint but I want
everybody to know I'm coming and I got the freedom
you ain't got though you got caddies and caddielacks
like I got cool freedom without my god and I'll not
shake your horny hand for the Poetry Police are still
coming to carry you all away and I'll blow my own way
my valley way like I'll blow cool as you blow up the
like-me world—'

But there was only myself riding along in an empty thirdclass carriage and the train bowling along hooting through ice-cream hills and refrigerated mountains and tunnels and battlements and thighs of valleys and skin of snow and the train generating existence as it blew its own way with its monster whistle through the lumbered forests of the night where all's cut down and we'll to the woods no more with sleep's whistles still blowing and so blow through blow in blow back blow down bow down so pause and begin again strike limb with joy again though the laurels be cut into board lengths and I lumbered over too and I a river without trees but still sweet river run down although my morning's choiceless Virgin dug me not or digs me not so wig me not with it for the dawn is coming and my voice did spend the night alone in my body and wandered up to my mouth and came out small and cried somewhere for Out between tongue and teeth and the traveling mirror with its fixed stare still to be broken still to be cracked as love cracked me open and I fell through in the night and heard nothing because mirrors are not ears although full of echo and intricate music make my penis wake and love still try to fornicate and soul lie down between too late in a society organized to promote peotomy where still a penis trained to love shoots on in dream shoots off away past Geneva in morning sun with bright starched avenues and starched flags flying by a starched lake and starched clouds over the esplanade and the lake full of speedboats and swimmers and islands with bridges and birdsong on breakfast

terraces above the lake and roofs aslant in the sun on hillsides and morning laughter over water and a bathing-pier with soft flesh bodies sunning and sharpies running to dive to lie beside blond bodies and breasts rising and falling ah the ivory skin that breathes aie turn me on and it would cost her a groaning but I'll not fall off here I've longer roadbeds still and an anonymous body on a hot beach attesting to the anatomical identity of historical woman makes me not fall off here to paint a novel in Geneva language though she wear the key to a community between her breasts and she lie alone at the end of a pier by a lighthouse with a towel around her head asleep almost with her breasts rising and falling a wood cross between them and the face hidden in its towel to pose a question of identity as if she did not own those breasts I recognize and the face I recognize but have never seen suffering its connèction with the body as on the Pont du Mont Blanc the canton flags are dancing and the final island like a cork in the bottleneck of the lake where the bottled water falls down and River Rhone flows out into another country and the swans still on the still water above the dam by the island with its gravel paths wood benches shade trees and birds all drifting toward the waterfall and falling in watered sunshine and I falling with it for I have climbed up here to fall and climb to fall heels over head and leaded feet all whelmed away as waterwheels turn en route and generate power that is not love though it generate existence itself as the wheeling train still generates the landscape before it and each instant being born in
98

gestures of trees houses animals sprung up like the long grass sprung up by the tracks that themselves grow before the engine as Spring puts forth again its old rumor of immortality and triumph over death as man himself arises from the dead when he is born and so falls headlong into another country past monasteries hung in hills with monks and celibate St. Bernard dogs rescuing snowlost people fallen out of Simplon tunnels and not all conductors priests on the Holy Year Express to Rome on which I go flying through the fated air but feel-me-not for I am brave to feel myself and see myself and see for myself what cooks below and need no Dante guide no Cook's low tour of the netherlands for I would cook my own down there and eat my own fat stew that *pot-au-feu* I throw all fodder in and the tour train full of French Italian and Swiss students and Venice floating by by night and all arrested there for a stop at the edge of the stones of Venice.

And those stones all loaves of bread and the gondolas with prows like coxcombs tilting by and the bridges made of runnels of bulged crust over the flowing dough of canals and in a bent square the size of a football field the billion hibernating souls of pigeons flock for holey bread and a gesticulating waiter pushes me excitedly into a chair and throws a sheet around my neck and starts stuffing pizzas down my neck and pouring basketbottles of wine on me all the while singing and laughing and waving his arms and shouting side remarks to a fat woman who sits watching me from the far side of the open-air restaurant and urging me on to eat and drink and assenting wildly and loudly to everything the waiter proposes laughing hysterically and screaming Yes! Yes! every time he brings me a new bottle and finally when I can make it no longer she comes running over to me still shouting Yes Yes and drags me off into a smaller courtyard and then into a smaller courtyard that leads into a smaller courtyard that leads into a smaller courtyard that leads into a smaller courtyard that leads into a still smaller courtyard that leads into a still smaller courtyard where windup phonographs are playing that lead into a still smaller darker court which leads into a still darker court that leads into a still blacker and closer court but someone left the record on and it's stuck and still turning over and over the same phrase and the still smaller and smaller and darker courtyard revolving and revolving with the record as I revolve and revolve with it turning and turning through the pigeon air as the huge one with pneumatic breasts and promise of pneumatic bliss leads me on up and up a stone stair that turns and turns in pumice air as myriad birds also ascend and turn and turn around it as I climb and the whole history of climbing to be found in the slippery moss of poetry on prose stairs and the whole story of climbing and falling through time to love is a story of a tower that narrows and narrows as I climb through a life and a land where the law of gravity can never be repealed and the sequel to climbing is certain as dingdong death but still up the corkscrew ladder I go and I've not been able to keep up with the fleeting image before me that grows thin-

100

ner and thinner and more ideal in shape the further she
gets away from me until she disappears completely in
the romantic haze and now I see only a woman with a
carrot head leaning out and beckoning me from a top
floor window of a dank hotel that leans out over the top
of the tower I've climbed and her head waggles as if
swaying on the end of a stick and winks at me and
laughs and dodges in behind crumby curtains as I stare
up through ivory glare of a moon that paints ideal features over the actual torn fabric of the disappearing
face and when the head dodges out again from behind
its curtains it has become like the upsidedown reflection
in a mirror curved inward with lean drawn features
stretched as if by weights hanging down from the top
of the head but the weights are actually her hair and
the head's eyes look down through it for an instant and
then dodge out of sight again as if afraid I would see too
deep and too much beneath the smiling painted fabric
but 'too deep and too much' was exactly what I thought
I wanted to see as if it were the only way to see any
reality and so I jump off my tower and over the rooftops
into a window of that leaning hotel and so start climbing up through *its* stories in a continuation of the story
of my life of climbing and falling but I waddled and
sweated too much as I came and at each landing heard
the thirst quenchless flushing of bidets and glimpsed
through halfclosed doors the Bosch-like bodies of groan-
ers struck motionless in postures of love which were
not love itself and at each higher landing up the narrowing spiral stairwell I looked through keyholes

101

that had no community keys and saw the bodies that assumed more and more passionate frenzied gestures and postures imitating love with their voices rising and rising into hungrier and hungrier wailing after the love they did not find in the act of it until at last the whole sound of that striving fell away on the very top floor of that building and that sound shrank into one wheezing toothless laugh issuing from the throat of a fiftynine pound woman midget with long hair whose head was the actual one I had seen from below and who now came waddling toward me in rubber slippers and a green gauze kimono under which fleshcolored Falsies jiggled and fell out and she is the shrunk shell of a once-famous and beautiful fandango dancer known as La Bella Muchacha and she is all salami dancing for my head and she wears veils through which desire looks and cries and she dances in my head but she wants more than my head she wants my body on a spit as the sweet night swings and sings her breasts my valley where I find my song and Venice below in the night undulating like a huge painting in a swaying frame and my cockscomb gondola swaying in it and the tour train now blowing its high hollow whistle again.

So hurtling out across the lost blue plains and Giotto landscapes in night and traintime whirling on through the Roman country on invisible wheels and out into day again and past Fiesole in sun and past Florence crooking its river and past a woman with the same face hidden in a towel of a veil waving from a bridge the white hand hung

in sun and reflected upsidedown in the river and a syl-
lable of a sybil of a golden branch caught in the hand
and that branch a key of a golden bough that turned in
the sun of fertility and was a key to an underworld of
acts of love where love itself was never mentioned while
still traintime whirled and flashed past wheelless and
the train turned into an orangecrate-local rocking and
bulging with country pilgrims and more and more of
them crowding on at every drag stop in the Roman
country with everybody shouting and crying and pushing for a seat or hanging on through windows and this
whole flying circus scene flying on toward Rome with a
tick tick on mindless rails as day falls into night again
and in a side strain of a main drain from a side train to
the main train at a lonely country crossing a flax-haired
farmgirl mounts my wooden carriage which is already
stuffed full with hot pressed humanity but she squeezes
in and is pushed tight in front of me and then squashed
down in my lap and my key turns and she is looking
without knowing for that lost community and all
wedged in so tight that none can move and she has a
rooster in a sack and it bites my ear and in the wheeling
dark the world is all keys and keyholes the world is a
set of fantastic keyholes in the doors of dark people in
the doors of dark men and straw-haired women and
they all Dante's muddy people beautiful in the swart
moving dark of their descending journey over the night-
black plains descending through seven circles and
Dante that eternal tourist in Hell who followed the
conducted tour with various official state department
103

guides who always kept him strictly within the officially prescribed itineraries never allowing him to wander astray into restricted defense plant areas or other top-secret projects of the Devil that he plotted out on special proving-grounds and never allowing Dante to poke about by himself because he was an unofficial observer from whose jockstrap dangled the one true key of love that could unlock all the doors of the seven stages of Heaven and Hell if he but realized he carried that masterkey upon his own person but I had the key and here was a hole and I turned it again and I gently bit that farmgirl's ear and she turned her head in the dark and feels with her hand to find what it was and finds my face with her hand and her fingers find my lips and I kiss them as she withdraws her hand and I bite her ear again very gently and feel a quick intake of breath and I kiss the lobe of her ear and kiss her neck beneath it and to kiss was to love and she would not and she would not have me stop yet pulls away and turns her face to mine and cannot see it in the rocking dark and my lips catch her open mouth and she strains away yet now not away and her breath hot in my mouth her tongue meeting mine before she breaks away again gasping but then her mouth comes back and fastens itself on mine and to kiss was to love in most mythologies and a kiss was a turn of a lock though the lock knew not what turned it and the key a skeleton key that turned in doors it never knew and she wanting no answer except the answer of my lips and wants no answer but the taste of them and wants no voice from them except the breath of them and would not let me stop that answer riding in the dark and pressing down on me riding me in swaying carriage motion where all slept around us in the dark as heavyheaded trees flash by and she takes both my hands and presses them around her breasts up under the hot wool the bursting breasts with nipples hard and hungering as she would never let me go if I would never stop as now she trembles in her skin and moans in pressing down on me until I too and night and hot I yes and riverrun and Tiber run down to the sea in overflowing tenderness as that long night flowed on across the Roman countryside and it was the string I was always stealing and where did the string lead then when with a sudden jerk the couplings break and something in the wheels is broken or tangled and all grinds to a halt in time and place way out nowhere in the country and the awakened passengers now all piling out along the tracks to watch repairs by lanternlights with brakemen voices underneath the car and the black fields about standing lost forever in their own eternity and bats part of it flitting over dark banks and grass like hot hair we find to sit upon away from the others beyond the lights and stretched out on it then and so lay still like that she pulled me over her my mouth on hers she would not let me move how long we lay like that where the wind moved until together trembling again at last and finally the broke train blowing again hitched up to go once more as we stagger up and run for it and catch our moving car and scramble in and so ride on toward Rome and so come out in Rome dismounting and dissembling past exhausted torsos of engines and each engine with its one great illuminated eye poking itself out through the station which is one of the seven stations of Rome and at the great swing doors of this station is a holywater stoup as if this were no railroad exit but one of the seven church entrances to the crossfigured city and my tour ticket included one free drop of holywater which the eternal tickettaker at the gate gives me in the form of a tear as I pass out and the drop of water on my forehead the tear on my forehead is a pearl of sweat at the base of the sign of a cross that a hand drew on my head and on my skin which I was still inside of was not yet out of could not get out of and I could not remove that tear though it ran down to the end of my nose and hung there suspended because I was afraid someone would see me if I tried to wipe it away and I was afraid to remove it for it was not water but blood it was a drop of blood at the end of my nose although I could not tell whether or not it was my own but I at last sniffed it up and it tasted like my own blood and had that familiar unfamiliar taste which is the taste of one's own blood not tasted before and in this pellmell flowing of my blood out of that strain I had lost the girl in it I had lost her anonymous body in the flow of myself I had absorbed her into my blood and could not see her any more as the eye could not see itself as I fell out into the crossfigured cave of Rome through jungles of tenements overhead trolleylines owls and madonnas.

And I had either a female owl or madonna or a swan or a female pigeon under my arm or in a sack and this pigeon or swan or dove had the most beautiful breast which I kept stroking and she kept pecking and kissing the lobe of my ear and was only as imaginary as the crazy sad bird I carried around in my head as the idea of woman and which still turned and turned every whichway and sang and turned and was the parrot of love who kept repeating all the phrases and phases of it and turned and turned on its pedestal which was my head and stood on my head and gripped my head with its talons and made little creases in my face with its claws and went on singing its wiggy little sexy song and kept on growing larger and larger until my head could not contain it any longer and could not carry it any longer and I had to carry that bird in a sack instead and even this growing unmanageable after a while since that bird was constantly growing madder and madder and so now we were caught up in a pilgrim procession of praying arms and legs in a sea of eyes and lips chanting Latin phrases over the desert concrete that wound through paper streets and up papyrus avenues which were the wrinkled pages of a breathing Bible which was the original beat blackbook of humanity and all wound straight to the Colosseum in a great Holy Year parade of students at midnight and all of them shouting 'Goal! Goal! Touchdown!' and the white ruins of the Colosseum lit by torches and the great mob parading in and around it waving torches and singing and the whole stone womb of it filled with gesticulating arms and legs and waves of bodies like rushing water and the two of us that is to

107

say that bird and myself floated up and up on the crest
of those human waters to the top of the amphitheatre on
great stone steps at its topmost rim where nightlocked
on shingle wings great bats flew about and the great
crowd settling down below like a sea sinking into crenelated earth and the two of us left flapping about up
there on the dark stone and we were stranded on a small
island of stone by the receding tide and we had lost the
power of flight although we still had wings and they
were putting all the torches out down below and a huge
hush was descending on the now-sitting multitude for
it was almost the midnight moment when the Pope was
to address the mob on loudspeakers from Vatican City
and the Colosseum was some kind of waitingroom outside some Health Plan center not endowed by a ruined
trillionaire where a million impatient patients waited
without their Health Plan cards to get into where
Health Plan nurses circulated in white hoods and the
head dictor the head doctor was coming to make his
rounds the chief consulting physician-in-residence was
coming to make his ministry among them and among
the lovers and weepers who were all one and each telling his lover he himself was not god yes each lover
telling his lover he is not god although each lover might
be god in the act of love and the hero vulnerable wears
no pants at night and we alone up there at the top of
the world under the inky burning sky and we could no
longer fly because something had happened to our
wings yes my wings had atrophied from lack of flying
and I had only vestigial remains of wings in the lobes

of my ears which my twin bird kept nuzzling and I was
a curious kind of great fat seabird who had somehow
tried to mate with a beautiful white pigeon or dove
from another archipelago and I was making love to that
feathered idea and I was stroking her breast as her
wings beat about me but my illusions were shrinking
and we were no longer fair birds but realistic bees
perched on the rim of a hive filled with thousands and
thousands of drones and young queens and this hive of
the Colosseum was like one of those castles of German
legend whose crenelated walls are composed of myriad
phials containing the souls of men about to be born in
an abode of life that precedes life and the 'queen-bee'
now took off above me and soared straight up into the
dark blue looking for the sun without which she could
not mate and I am climbing after her and she soars so
high into the infinite opal that eventually the sun re-
appears on the far side of the world and it is at that
infinite height that I seize her and the two of us bound
further aloft with renewed impetus and the ascending
spiral of our intertwined flight whirls for one second in
a hostile climactic madness of love but no sooner is the
union accomplished than my abdomen opens and my
organ detaches itself dragging with it the mass of my
entrails and the wings relax and as though struck by
lightning the emptied body turns and turns on itself
and sinks back and back to the abyss below and the
'queen-bee' too then descends and descends from the
azure trailing behind her like an oriflamme the unfolded
entrails of her lover the murderous tokens of impregna-

tion and the 'queen' falls finally down into the center of
the Colosseum hive and there is divested by drones of
the embarrassing souvenirs her lover has left her and
retains only the seminal liquid from which over the years
will issue millions of eggs from which will spring to life
a whole race since she has within her an inexhaustible
male although by a curious inversion it is the queen
who furnishes the male principle in ovulation and the
drone the female and that drone of myself whose organ
was contrived by nature only to function in space has
now accomplished his admirable ecstasy and falls bleeding to death like an artist who has finally and fatally
succeeded in killing the romantic within himself and
his art and this element once killed never able to rise
again in the air and stuck to earth forever afterward can
only make love lying on the hard stone of it with the
weight of his grave body pressing down on top of the
body of any other lover he can come upon and that
lover no more than some substitute 'queen' which he
nevertheless still presses to earth and will never let up
and will never allow to escape from his hot breath
which is still the breath of illusion in which he is perpetually coming and coming and coming and coming and
the Pope speaking over Saint Peter's loudspeakers filling
the air with His voice as all fall down as all that had
risen as all who had risen fell down before Him as all
who had risen there for His coming now fell down upon
their blisters of knees and then all falling finally away
and the Colosseum crumbling away before Him and
myself also fallen and falling away through the pouring

110

crowd of exodus with relit torches and the terrible anonymity of that other animal body I had loved up there now floated away from me for good and redissolved itself in that sea of animal love which existed at a constant level and redifferentiated itself ceaselessly in myriad animal bodies and re-articulated itself ceaselessly in eyes and lips and the reforming procession of those bodies now pouring out into the sleepless city and crumbling away into the cracks of the city in which I now found myself wandering around and around a dark square in which the Pantheon crouched.

And it was the same old scene all over again as if I had never left Paris and myself still gooking about among old monuments statues and clichés in cities I had never left with their famous places and squares and streets all recapitulating the same bopless baedeker banalities with the place and the street-names changed but the same creepy nowhere hero making his mushy exiled rounds the same walking cliché never able to break away into the free air of underivative creation like some sculptor perpetually enrolled at the American Academy in Rome forever sketching the sculptured classic head of a pantheon lion rather than the lion's hard hidden balls and still carrying within him not only all the Cook's tour places of his exile but also some anonymous doll idol or dumb dancing *poupée intérieure* on a string. But I had had enough of all that. Now, finally, I'd had enough. Now I'd stop at last. Yes, that was it, just stop drooling all that neoclassic mush, just pause and begin again, with a new

111

clean sketchbook not scribbled all over with anonymous figures, no more dark Helens with blind eyes staring out of classic ruins. Over and over again I came to the same point on the paper or canvas—I made one nice clean underivative line, and there it was ready to be made into 'something new,' my brush or pencil poised over it ready to enact the new, but what came, what resulted? The brush came down, lost itself, made the old face, the drippy paint fell back into its old habits, sticking to everything, to the old forms. I thinned it out with turpentine, but still it stuck, I never got the brushes clean of it, never got the canvas scraped clean, for the old lead would not scrape off, I could never bear to scrape it off completely, I was afraid of the bare bones or of the bare void I imagined was all that existed in the fiber of the canvas itself.

There was a light in a window, a light in a tall window on the first floor of a stone hotel that looked like a temple across the square. I went toward it, stopped myself halfway, for there I'd gone again straight into old abstractions, seeing that stone building as a temple. It wasn't a temple, it was merely some old hotel. I pulled a cord at the door. I still had to sleep somewhere, as if I hadn't been asleep all this time. I pulled the cord again, heard a tinkle bell inside. Still nobody came to the door. Then a shadow moved at last in the lighted window, and the two halves of the window pushed out. A woman's voice called. It was unmistakably an American voice. I said, 'Are there any rooms—I was looking for a room—' Silence. After a while I could hear the big wood door being unbolted, opened, the same flat voice saying 'The Signora's gone out—but—you could wait—' I stepped in through the great doors, came face to face with a tall girl in the stone hall. She wore a long wool scarf wound around her neck and down her back, as if she'd been trying to keep warm in a cold room. She looked at my face, pushing her straight hair back from her forehead, repeated, 'Yes, there're rooms—' and stopped, undecided, looked in my face again, brushed her hair back again. 'I was making some tea—would you like some tea—while you wait?' When I nodded, she turned and walked in a sloping stride down the long hall, and I followed her into her high room where a small coal fire burned on an enormous bare hearth, with a tin teapot on it. A book lay open on the floor. And so it began again. I looked at that face, would turn my 'key,' but it did not turn so easily as all that, a more complicated mechanism inside, more locks and bolts to be drawn before any turning. And instead of beginning in dream and voyaging off into the actual world and then returning afterward to dream, I would this time begin with the real and stick to it, voyage nowhere out of it. Here was a tall thin girl whose 'reality' was strange enough without shadows, standing in front of the tiny fire, clutching her elbows as if still trying to get warm, her black hair cut short, hanging straight down around a curiously egg-shaped little face that seemed to have come out of an old painting by Hieronymus Bosch. No, that wasn't it. Instead of a hazy image out of somebody else's painting or out of my own, I saw

113

this girl in sharp outline, a clear, incisive line, the oval head on its long stalk like a curious turning almond-flower. She wore no lipstick, no jewelry. She had long thin hands, the fingers almost spatulate. . . .

And how long, then, did I spend in that hotel, in an identical bare room on the floor above, with a tenfoot high window over a long windowseat— One night and day and another night, perhaps more. Memory was the real painter, and it foreshortened everything in that Roman canvas, crushing days into hours and minutes, events that took a long time to happen pressed together, hilltops of sensation brought together and heightened by the elimination of time between them. It was evening, it was morning, the yellow light moved along the tile of the floor, she sat still in a straight chair, I on the edge of the windowseat, looking out. Beside the long couch and a big armoire, there was only one other piece of furniture, her straight chair with fluted back, and it near the bare fireplace, almost directly under a single hanging light. She sat with her long legs crossed and bent slightly sideways by the weight of her elbow that rested on one knee, with one hand cupping her chin, her head tilted to one side, her eyes upon the book. She was older than myself, perhaps thirty, or thirty-two. Or thirty-five. Hard to tell. Why was she there, in a single stone room in Rome, by herself? She did not know why she was there, or at least would not say why she had come. She had come direct from the States, by a slow Greek boat, landing at Genoa, a week, two weeks before. It was her

114

first trip abroad, and when later we went out together into the city for the first time, she moved among the monuments, an old 1910 Baedeker in hand, but as if not so much studying-out the plan of a vanished city as puzzling over some mislaid scheme of her own life. Boygaited, she moved in a sloping walk which one might have mistaken for sleepwalking, yet I felt she missed nothing, saw the birds rise from the walk, fly over, noted the flick of light on leaves that quivered, wondering about them too, catching the glint of a bicyclist's eye as he flicked by, or the bright flight of hats down a street, or a bunch of drip-dry shirts hurrying home from offices, or the tail of a dog just disappearing round a corner ahead of us, as if she photographed everything as she went and stored it up inside in a file that was not disorderly yet took no account of categories and classifications of things or of the outer shapes of people. I saw her as thin and very tall; she did not see me as squat and fat. So I thought. But it was in her room that she let me sketch her, sitting in her chair in that characteristic position, reading, head cocked just slightly as if contemplating some curious question that had just occurred to her, or that recurred and recurred, from time to time brushing a straight lock back from her forehead with a quick nervous motion and a slight shake of her head. Her eyes would continue across the page very slowly, not as others read for details but in the same way she looked at monuments or trees, to uncover some scheme of things that might very possibly be discovered in the gesture of a thing or in the turn of a phrase on the page.

It was natural, then, that she should read poetry—or books of prose by poets. She rose once and came over to show me the book she was reading then, handing it to me as if it were a piece of her life.

It was a certain H.D.'s *Palimpsest*, a prose book but a purple book, with ivory paper. She left me with it, went over to the fireplace, roused the coal fire as I read, straightened up, brushing the hair from her face, looking across at me, clutching her elbows lightly to her sides. Her fire was always going out, she was always trying to rekindle it, she had been trying to keep warm all her life, and she had handed me the book as if I would find her in it, or at least explain something of herself to me which she would not put into words. The words were incised in the white skin of the pages, as if in marble, English words, yet clean and hard as Greek lettering on a lintel. I read. . . . *Her face . . . stark . . . intense . . . the close cowl of strange hair . . . Her laugh . . . the girl was not awakened. . . . And he had only to wait to bring to the thin, rather colourless lips the stark agonizing cry for pity that would finally prove Rome the conqueror . . . aie, aie . . . He wanted . . . to cause her finally and distinctly to commit herself. . . . But she did not give him satisfaction. . . . He saw woman, not a line (searing the soul, inflaming the spirit, scarring the mentality) . . . She was, he regarded her, an idea, an obsession. . . . She was something come to plague, to destroy . . . her tongue dwelling viciously (with an intensifying beauty on syllables she must have realized*
116

ate into him, scalded, flayed him) . . . taken parasitic
root in him . . . in her quest for perfect Attic verity.
. . . I'd read enough, I'd had enough of 'all that,' I did
not wish to become hung-up again on that old hook,
among the strange statues that moved and moved. Why
wouldn't anybody leave them alone, why did they have
to keep digging them up all the time, fishing them up
like lost urns out of the sea, over and over? The yellow
light moved along the tile, ran along the high ceiling,
a cloud passed over, she sat again in her chair, she rose
and came over, bent over to see where I read. I looked
up in her face, drew her head closer, it was evening,
clouds passed shadows on her face, darkened the al-
monds in them, passed over. At the last moment, she
avoided my lips, turned to sit sideways on the windowseat. She had come a long way from somewhere, in a
tight way of hunting, a knot of wanting. She could not
untie it, not untie herself, let loose, turn loose a bird
that beat everywhere in her with the tumult of myriad
caged wings. Or so I imagined, so I thought, putting the
book aside, raising a hand to her scarf, to unwind it
from her throat. She would not let me, seemed to shiver
in the warm air that blew in. I leaned out past her, drew
the double windows in, latched them, as she sat still.
Still leaning over her on that windowseat, I looked down
in her face, the eyes still shielding me out, cataracts
between us, I took her head in both my hands to make
her eyes meet mine more fully, a white light mask I held
in my hands, an alabaster cast made from a face, taken
from a face that had, I imagined, just recently come

117

from hysteria, and she did not stop me now as I loosened her scarf, kissed her throat and the hollows at the base of it, pushing her gently back and down upon the wood seat. A vein beat at the base of her throat, the skin transparent, purple-veined, and she let me open her blouse, kiss her breasts. First lights glinted through the window in the first of night, and she would not stop me, for I was somebody else to her, with a name like Noel, and her longing only to be appeased by that person who had originally made her long, and I could 'possess' her only as one 'takes' a photograph of another, taking only the image and imprint of the body and not whatever might be inside it. Or so I imagined, so I thought. As if we were a couple of anonymous bodies in that room, and her body no more than that famous *petit gâteau* which when dipped in a cup of tea and brought to the lips immediately evoked a whole former world and time of life when first that special little cake had been tasted, the whole involuntary memory of it now awakened and sprung to life again. It was the anonymous body itself which, when tasted, raised to life again by a kind of magic a thousand elements that had existed in me in fragmentary state and which were now re-united, assembled, joined together again, bridging every gap between them to form anew that first face. . . . But her book had fallen to the floor; a piece of string used for a marker lay beside it, curled. It was no longer pure white. A tiny streak of dirt ran along one side of it where it lay innocently enough. She lay still, with her eyes closed, and I was absolutely unable to move. I kept looking

down at her face and then at the book on the floor beside the seat and at the piece of string. The whole scene
began curiously turning, in my head. A horse with some
kind of carriage or wagon clomped by outside, its
shadow went over the wall, the room filled with horse
shadows, revolving, as on a carrousel platform or moving café terrace, and I was drowning in a maze of head-
less turning statues and horses. After a long while she
half-opened her eyes, turned her head, looked where I
was looking on the floor, reached out and down to retrieve the string and book, without raising herself,
started to put the book and string down on the edge of
the seat beside her. They slipped through her fingers
and lay on the floor again. She let them lie, closed her
eyes again, lay still again, waiting and not waiting, a
photograph that had to be taken before the film got too
old to be developed. The horses had all marched away
along the walls, and one of them had left a very small
streak of mud along one of her cheeks, or perhaps it was
just a leftover shadow, or—no, it was a kind of a hoof-
print upon her skin, just above where the swelling of
her breasts began—no, it was not a footprint, it was a
print or a shadow of a very small cross, white against
the surrounding skin, as if the sun had—no, there was
nothing, all was shadow. She shivered almost imper-
ceptibly now, her skin become cool marble, purple-
veined, incapable of being warmed, her life an attempt
to get warm, I had only to awaken her fully . . . only
to bring to those lips . . . the girl was not awakened
. . . But I'd had enough of that. If only she too had had

119

enough of that book, with its classic girl 'forever unpossessed' in her quest for 'perfect Attic verity' which might have truly been the Greek ideal yet still was all statues that moved, shadow upon shadow, web upon web of illusion. Or so I thought, just as the dumb hero of that book had thought. Ruminated, rather. I could ruminate with the best of them. And at moments like this. Too much 'thinking' ruined it all, words, in their quest for Attic verity, were the real destroyers, the real preventors, each a little fence. And I had had my own obsessions. Somewhere in the interior of the building a toilet flushed. There had been a light at a window, a white face in it, white as the bleached skull of a cow. She'd turned my bed down, a blue bed, sun went away, a sweet tongue spoke in my sleep, a brass ball shone. Rang. With light. That room did not last long. Gone, with a dingdong bell. A slow, low bell, a single bell. Thud. She'd held an asphodel, the brass bell tolled, with a dead sound. It rolled in the street, it rolled around the world, it was morning. We'd rolled apart, and I'd slept and dreamt that a dark, muffled figure opened my door, with a special key, and nothing in that room but the promise of her nearness, unowned by anyone in the world, and we flowed into each other, as all human lives flowed into each other, and I dreamt that this girl cried in sleep, that her tears had held her words together and made them flow, she not able to hold back the words which, when awake, she would not speak. Now I looked down at her still sleeping face, and still heard those words, clear, incised as on a lintel, heard her speak them

120

separately but could not now put them together into any sense. What I had half-apprehended about her in sleep had now, in waking, entirely escaped me. Now all I saw was a curiously egg-shaped little face, a hung-up girl on a string, and I fell asleep again and she was not in it, nor in the clomp of a passing horse, nor in the gray air that flooded in, nor in the trains that ran, nor in the rain that fell, nor in the sound of phonographs turning and turning. Bidets and subway toilets constantly flushed and it was another flood I was in and people swam from each other over all horizons, all taken by a new form of Piblokto madness, a new violent form which did not allow the victims to come into the slightest contact, mental or physical, with anyone else, neither male nor female. When I finally awoke, it was past noon. She was gone from the windowseat, from the room, from Rome for all I knew, for there was a note on the mantel, and I could not piece together the strict, gracile lettering into any real sense. I was surprised to see how small her writing was, like little pigeon or gull tracks leaning backwards across the page, making a little bent path. Noncommittal, betraying nothing of herself in relation to me, each word turned about upon itself and wandered about by itself, as if fallen off some high lintel or pedestal. They did not say where she had gone, only that she would not come back. The room, not very much emptier than when it had contained her body, now seemed larger, higher, stonier, hollower. The square outside, like the room, seemed to have expanded and was full of large, empty sounds. The boulevard beyond

121

was bent like a rubberband that stretched and snapped, curling upon itself. The streets beyond curled away, deserted, everyone having run away from each other, afraid of each other in the final Piblokto madness. Mistaking the deserted temples of Rome for deaf mutes, I clapped my hands to awaken them, my claps bouncing back like thrown stones, except at one temple where Tenebrae still groaned and Lent's long night-mass still went on all day, and where from the arched door I saw one woman left among the dark pews, a figure I thought I recognized, her face hidden in a lace mantilla. She felt my look on her, turned her head upon its stem. O dark of hair. Clay asphodel. Her eyes, made of mascara, looked into mine over an immense distance in which nothing else existed—yet in an instant passed over me, recognizing nothing. I fell back into the still street that wound away, out of the city. Along the Appian Way, among the dark pines and shattered shadows, a nightingale resumed, indistinctly, incessantly, stopped and resumed in the still dusk. In a pine grove by the Villa Borghese, children were playing, imitating marching soldiers and battles, twittering and shrieking like swallows, at evening. And they disappeared. There was a thrill in the air. A voice among the trees was calling. Not 'her' voice. A phallic voice beyond the world, above, beyond the trees, a hidden brilliance. . . .

III

A light in a window, a high light, a skylight filled with sun and cinders, a courtyard filled with watered light, someone filling it with a garden hose. Ants in my eyes. I blinked and they went away. *Vitrier!* But distantly. Down away, in the Rue du Cherche Midi. And back. I was back, had gone nowhere out of myself, though in a nightmaze sleep I'd waded through three continents, polyphoboisterous and singing to myself in the drunk bateaux of sleep's trains all marked Home and sheeted in oblivion in the final tunnel of the hole in my wall. The old hole. Still there. I still in it. In my cracked mirror. I was looking into it, my face fixed like a mask upon the wall. It was not the mirror that was cracked. There were only cracks where my image was. It was not I that changed, it was the world. From time to time I stroke the sides of my nose with the edge of a hand that appeared dead, whose fingers were oddly stiff and distended, almost spatulate. And someone had been drawing spiderwebs on my face, with a feather. Or with a very small comb, a celluloid comb. And what was that eminence? My hat, I had forgotten to remove my hat, had slept in my hat, had come back from a long journey and had not yet removed my hat, for I was not going to stay. That was it, must have been it. It must have been in the back of my mind, on the back of my head.

I'd out again, with my hat to cover my hole, the little porthole of myself, but in the back streets of that port-city the harbor did not exist, and my back streets the back streets of Saint-Sulpice, to which in a series of wandering circles I returned, the square alive with a whirring of pigeons, beating about my head, in the stone gallery of a street with a door with a cigarette light in its mouth from which I made no progress away. I was to say I already paid, we'll not mention the fee, and dawn caught me, light bred, the great I of a gothic tower rose, far over, on the Ile de la Cité. Night-held, I imagined the figure of the Virgin. Caryatid. A dance figure. Asphodel again. I'd go that way, yet not that way. Bits of wreckage, cornerstones, lampposts adrift, blown posters, a bird, a shadow, a dark sound, and the wind came up like a gale of tongues, sweeping up a sleeping cat, a crumpled copy of *L'Humanité*, a wandered statue of a distant man. Somewhere a madman shook a black flower, the fourth person singular shaking a black flower. Or an asphodel. In paper sky. Street-sweepers coming, swept me before them, down the Rue de Seine, out into the Place Saint-Germain, its church locked and barred, stone tilted tower with twisted apse propped in paper air, wind shoe-ing me on, down the Rue Bonaparte, toward the river. They had rolled my life in a cave and put a stone in front, and I read it all in a drifted paper which I did not dare pick up. I ran along after it, reading the paper as we skittered on, my life printed there, with a picture of my head in the square black frame of a mirror. I saw my life drifting in gutters, lying torn on the floor of lavatories, lining garbage cans, saw it wrapped around a fish in the hands of a Brooklyn fishmonger, saw it fresh and clean on a windy winter morning on a sidewalk newsstand in Brooklyn, saw it being printed years in advance of publication. Why had they written it all out and set it in type and filed it away in galleys long before, years before its publication? Written in the fourth person singular, it was very clear, very accurate, there was no need to rewrite it when the time came to publish it. All they'd had to do at the last moment was add a single paragraph, write a lead for it all. I could not make it out, I reached down for it.

My hand could not reach it. There was something wrong with my hand. It was very dirty. If earth was dirty. The nails had grown long. They were the color of roots. They were roots. Someone had planted me. I was growing in the ground. I saw my feet for the first time. The nails had broken through the toes of my shoes and were growing straight out, and they were the color of roots. My whole body was growing. I felt my face. It too was growing. It was becoming another face. Along the quais of the Seine, along the Quai Malaquais wind swept me in breathing bursts, down to the water. I could recognize my face in the sweat of the water. It was covered with small, flowing wrinkles, little cracks in every direction, from the corners of the eyes to the ears, from the corners of the mouth to the nose, from the corners of the nose into the cheeks, from the bottoms of the cheeks to the bottom of my chin. The brow was furrowed, for someone had been dragging the surface of the earth with a very small plow, and there were other cracks in my face, regular splits, as in the badly cracked mirror I had traded to the glazier. It had come back on the waters, its cracks the breaks on its surface, sliding, changing, everything still growing. I felt my eyes. Or rather I felt the sockets. The eyes themselves seemed not to be there at all. No, there they were, the pupils had simply dissolved, making the eyes appear empty. It was just that they were so clear that they looked empty. Like the eyes of municipal statues in small villages, the green leprosy of moss spreading over them. My eyes like that. They saw everything, had seen everything, understood nothing. But I could not see *with* them any more. Something was in the way. Ah, it was tears. My eyes were crying, foolish creatures. I heard the water's flooded crying, the river flooded high with Spring rains, whirled

126

and tossed. I was on a bridge, over a parapet, hanging out over the water, the water flooding from my eyes, my eyes which could see everything and had understood nothing and now could not see because of the water. I had B.O. of the soul, and the water rushed down to wash me off, down and under. Cold images in it. The water ran into the sea, everything ended in water, the sea flooded the world, broke and cried on goldrock shores, seastruck towers fell, the eaten shores collapsed, and sea rushed in where it could. All crumbled but all sprung to life again in my eyes. A root sprouted, a root had sprouted out of the corner of one eye. It had been a crow's crooked foot but it grew longer, hornier, sprouted feelers, branches, and became a root. A root on a crow, growing from a crow. The crow's claw hooked in the corner of my eye, among other crow's feet that grew and grew into new roots, spread over my face, down my neck, down my body. There was a great big vine sprouting out of the center of my body, there were twin shrubs growing from my breasts, a tree with a single root sprouting from my crotch. The great vine at the center of my body came out of my navel. The navel cord had become untied, in spite of all. Someone had untied it, and it was growing again, as it had before birth. Someone who had obviously known what to do. It was better to say Someone with a capital S, just in case. One never knew. Someone was pulling that vine again. It was attached to someone else again. A great body I was inside of. No, not yet inside of. She who would give birth to me was still a virgin. She was still to conceive me but she would give birth to me in the end. The dawn thickening like milk. In a body. Milk forming in a body, in the breast of a pregnant body that had yet to conceive. A river of milk rushing by, under the bridges, endless, flooding, crying like a baby. I was growing into something bigger, more diffuse. My face, becoming another face, was becoming fatter still. It became like the mold of a face, the kind sculptors used to pour a face. A new face was being poured for me, but so far there was only the mold of it. The mold grew on my face, like the green leprosy that attacked bronze statues in the gardens of the Musée Rodin. The mold now covered the whole of my face, and when it was completely covered, they would be ready to pore the face. No, the face was already pored and pockmarked and freckled. They would, rather, be ready to pour it, in the new mold that was forming, a mold of mind. The mold for the whole brain had to be regrown before the new brain could be poured. The old cells were breaking up, disintegrating, but the new ones would form out of the same stuff, out of the same material, into different crenelations, a different labyrinth, but with the same kind of ant crawling through it, though not precisely the same ant. For this little lonely ant of consciousness was not quite the same in everyone. Some were more alive than others, some had longer feelers, longer legs than others. Some were white ants, but not all. And the ones that had black ants inside of them had black gods. My ant had crawled up into me through my umbilical cord. Or it might have entered any place else, for all I knew. My anus or nose.

Either was handy. In any case, it was now walking around in my brain, with its little black bulb head, its ticklers and pincers searching everywhere, going as fast as it could, on all sixes. It was not really trying to get anywhere, it was only trying to count its legs. And its feelers. By tapping them like bent blind men's canes, one after the other. Tap, tap at every crossing of thought, waving and waving a white or a black feeler ahead of him, more like a spider than an ant, a thread spinning out behind, winding away, trying to unravel, refind its first daylight, over a bridge here, onto this island in the city, a bull at the center of the labyrinth, as if I'd a thread to get out again, a thread to thread my way away, a spider way, a thin thread, a thin string, a white string wound away in knots, the end in a ring, in a nose, in a bull nose, or a pope's nose, on a pigeon, or a papal bull, and the vine still growing in me, I still growing, planted, long hair sprouting, hair all tangled, hair I'd still untangle, with my little pocketcomb, I'd comb the streets still, still comb it out on this island in the Seine, with its spindrift steeples, its Notre Dame, its bridges with early foot-passengers rushing. They don't see me, rush right through me, right over me, look right through me, as if I were some un-house-broken dog who left his small sins in dark corners, his 'calling cards' they would say, as I had left my sins in various corners, my fleshpaint *conneries,* graffiti on a dark door with a cigarette light.

My feet still tangled in shadows, I nevertheless seemed to be moving forward over the Ile de la Cité with a terrible hunger, a terrible urgency, but the day had decided not to begin after all, and an enormous thundercloud suddenly fell and enveloped the whole island in a midnight gloom, a Bad Friday gloom, and I was a survivor in it, having taken refuge in a round *pissoir,* as in a turret of a ship, a conning tower from which, standing in the conning position, I turned my eyes through white headlights that broke upon the turret like spray, a sad, round ship I was captain of, with a lunacy among revolving trees, horns and traffic whistles. Brakes and anchors ground, on an indescribable journey that had only begun, in a heavy sea fog, a heavy Channel fog that furled around lampposts, tented buildings, shrouding the early winking traffic along the quais toward Notre Dame where the flowermarkets were just opening, country vendors setting out great heavy harvests of lilacs, tulips, coquelicots, hollyhocks, heavy sheaves, fair field flowers on the cobbled stones of the quai. A daedal earth had done it, a womb had made it, a girl had held her womb open, a hunger had come out, a terrible hunger of earth that turned and turned with its hungry horses that went round and round and up and down at the same time, each on its pole that would not let it go. It ran, and the ground whirled under it, and it became a dead camel on a turning *pissoir* of a merrygoround, going too fast for me to climb off of it, as I still reached out for lighted rings, rings of brass and rings of flowers. A flowerseller, a crone in a smock with gone teeth, leered and leaned out at me, thrusting a clutch of bloom at me as I passed. Coquelicots. Spring shook wings. *Coquelicots!* She screamed it, laughed a raucous laugh, her face blew away, the mad laugh continued in the fog, it was the sound of the laughing death that destroyed all islanders. Missionaries had reported it, in places like New Guinea. It afflicted only women and children and small dogs. They showed no disease organisms but suddenly became ill, wasted away, with their faces distorted in a Piblokto grin. They carried them away laughing like that, only then those who carried them became affected, and also began laughing like that, and also had to be carried away, by others who also became affected by the dead laughter, and also had to be accommodated on stretchers and carried away, until everyone not afflicted by this laughing had to be engaged fulltime in the manufacture of stretchers in which they themselves were soon to be carried away, although they were never carried quite far enough away, since those who carried them became victims and dropped the stretchers they were carrying, and it was all a curious relay-race in which the stretchers had to be picked up by someone new and carried a little further, until there was no one left to carry anyone, because everyone was on a stretcher, and all the stretchers lying out deserted on a great plain of earth with their passengers raising their arms feebly and motioning and signaling for someone to come and carry them onward, sticking their thumbs up in the sky as if they were trying to hitch-hike out of the world. And just what was this laughing sickness, after all? It wasn't a laughing sickness at all. I could see that plainly from the *pissoir* turret of my turning ship in the Seine. I could see plainly enough that this laughing was only a secondary symptom, a kind of protective coloring or instinctive reaction to cover up the real nature of the disease itself, to hide the real symptoms which involved a growing lack of actual communication between human beings. This was it exactly, and it grew at the root and heart of the matter like a large cancer that grew outward, eating all before it, yet remained perfectly hollow inside. The void of communication was growing, though I still heard whistles blowing in the fog and from time to time saw a headlight or a tree or heard a bell. Things were closing in, the fog was closing in more and more, until I couldn't see six feet in front of my turning conning tower. Everyone and every body was losing contact. Every body. That was it. Bodies were getting more and more out of contact with each other, though they were still used for making love. Making love was supposed to be a means of learning about love itself. As if there were a direct connection between love-making and love. A real connection between the two. Bodies were the connection, like the shuttle in a subway. Making love was a means of proving that life existed, a means of proving that love itself, spiritual love, was something that existed. Making love with bodies was a kind of speech to prove it, a language of being. Saints could prove it without bodies, I needed mine, needed to be in contact with other bodies, and so did everybody else on earth, and after a long while of wandering around trying to get in contact, to communicate with

132

others, everyone just finally gave up and started laughing and laughing. And they carried them off. That crone would not be back. But there she was again. Coquelicots! Back again, with a leer, with a cry, holding out the flowers toward me, as I whirled by in my merrygoround turret, turning on her profoundly gaudy smile, then a gaudy cackle, her lips without gums giving off an obscene sucking echo. Around again. I'd have to leave this *pissoir* of a ship sometime, I couldn't stay in the damn thing all morning, all day. If a French cop came by in the fog he would get suspicious, seeing me standing there forever and ever, in the conning position, shaking. One was supposed to finish one's business and be off, in a situation like that. No time for playing in there! They'd take you for a pervert of some kind, standing there with your feet and your hat showing, and a look of placid abstraction on the face. What could be going on in the middle, between the head, and the feet all this time? That's where everything happened in this world. One had to be careful, keep a check on things, call the gendarmes if things looked suspicious. A concierge in the Hotel Cluny Square used to sit in her room overlooking a corner with a *pissoir* on it, and whenever someone stayed in there too long, she'd call the flicks. Sure enough, they'd come. I'd have to watch out, time I was moving on, the fog lifting a little. Which way, though? Lost all sense of direction in this fog. Coquelicots! again, at a corner. What's that tower? Way over there. Notre Dame, no doubt. No, not Notre Dame. It's the Tour Saint-Jacques, across the river. I was looking

133

for Notre Dame and found the Tour Saint-Jacques instead, the tower without a church. Just what I needed, a tower without a church. Had all the advantages of a church without having to have the church itself. I could climb it, if I were really looking for a place to climb, I could benefit from its gothic aspiration, its leaping upward off the earth, to light. And without the drag of the body of the church attached, to drag me down in its pews. Coquelicots, again! Would she not leave me?

What was this *Devastatio* I was going through? Over and over. The flowered earth moving, the Spring wind breaking the fog, pushing me forward again, and now in the fog a permanent hole, a hole I knew, the seeing-eye of the fourth person singular that saw everything and understood nothing, yet still saw, the eye that saw and understood everything but myself, not able to see that in which it was itself imbedded, the fleshpaint skin I hid in like painters hiding behind their paint, authors behind their words, officers behind their uniforms, functionaries behind their functions, politicians behind their smiles and philosophers behind their pipes and everybody behind clothes, love behind bodies, beings behind flesh, the fleshpaint skin I laid on everything, having lied my life away in it, as if I were already twice my age, so many layers already unable to be peeled off, though under the dried skin of the paint was the still-wet body itself, and I had not heard the music stop, had not seen the skin slip off, the carapace drop away, the shredded fog fall off, not really wishing to regard the

134

hard underside and pelvis of love, and I had almost arrived at the place I did not really wish to go, and the
way up was the screwy way down, and I was to say I'd
already paid, I was to say that I was an immortality-
hunter, an Icarus flown over, and love to be achieved by
roasting the mean mind's sinews until they let loose
their tyrannical clench, or by the sprinkling of some
tenderizer directly upon the blind muscle, although tenderness of mind was not to be equated with love, and
love spelled backwards running into revolt and evolu-
tion, and a thought still able to revise the face of the
beloved, an eraser on its lines changing the drawn image, though the gum remained, the gum arabic remained, and I no weak-knee, no fly-by, no willow-way
drooling a clack of lacklove, no, not myself any more,
but another, and not mad, it's someone else that's always
mad, not my laughter that's mad, as they carry all away
with laughing sickness, but not me, for I'm my brother,
my lost long brother, in a brown robe and a brown rope
around me, my mind no slotmachine I ring, my lame
brain, my one-arm bandit, pull my arm and pull my leg
and pull the chain, flush out the old, ring in the new,
I'll be no looney-tom, no tit-willow dowager, no sweet
discalced with his plexus showing underneath his hem,
and yet, and yet I'll climb up there to be the lost astron-
omer who's studied the heavens all these years without
thinking of God, as if He were still squatting up there
beyond the range of our telescopes, having always to
move further and further away as the telescopes grew
longer, He, being absolute, having always to remain be-

yond the limits of vision, otherwise He'd no longer be infinitely infinite, and I yet to diagram my sentence in the final syntax and no way up but out and no way out but up in the dung time, the ash time, the dingdong time, the absolute zero of the year where the fooly phoenix rises out of Ash Wednesday, for I very much believe I don't believe, I believe and don't believe I believe, I don't believe and don't believe I don't believe, for I'm nowhere now, lost in the public domain, nowhere at all in this Channel fog. I should have stayed aboard my special ship, flying my own colors, instead of jumping off, into nowhere, all gone, all lost in it, everything forgotten.

Yet I'm still somebody, even if I'm nowhere. I'm a painter in a shingle shack on a far spit at tide's end at nightfall, trying to produce a world's face from the composite face of many people and painting one long picture all my life, sitting alone at a wooden table throwing bread to hordes of pigeons that come home at last, out of the set sun, and each crumb I throw is a broken drawing of one of them, and I'll yet go where the wind begins, I'll yet sail away on it, for I'm a ratio at the bridge of time and see flashes of my own beauty upon a bleak worldscreen, I'm on the inside of an egg, its shell my sensorium, where all's flashed as on a circular movie screen, but who's rolling the egg, who's rocking, what's really shaking, what's blowing, rolling me along, a round egg in a square world, a fat blob of an egg, blob upon the landscape, Lardy the Loser with a winning sweepstakes ticket, young Red Raffine the red herring, Crisco fat in the can come home again in the last race and so lie down in dark to be someone and walk away through the valley of my puttyball shadow, a lumpkin shadow, a bustard boy, a fortalice, Roman candle fizzled up a corkscrew stair and climbing a heaven that looks like hell, for I've an obsession with climbing and falling, a Quasimodo fear of high places, so scupper me not, drain me not through your gargoyle waterspout, romantic handle of a climbing root, brave root pecker, sweet worm that wastes away and falls, my old earth turner, young fish finder, hot diviner hung on me, my own divining rod that points both up and down, a phoenix in fog and dada bum descending, a *noyé pensif* who descends and who is roly-poly me, a sinking thinker, a thinking sinker, an ascending drowner sinking, who still would go through the toy fair or a fourth of July parade in a triumph of children firecrackers and laughter, and the almond tree still flourish and the grasshopper be a burden and desire fail as man goes on to his long home and the mourners go about the streets, someone always starting and stopping the film of it, winding and rewinding it, and everything proved by the slightest detail, everything reproved that needed no proving, the scene corresponding almost perfectly to reality, the coiled dark still unwinding, coming on, and Make mine vanilla cries the Queen and all starts over, for I'd still disarm her, unharm her, alarm her with those larmclock bells up there, or I'd turn back from here as lief as not as a leaf will fall before its time if someone shake the tree, and I'd turn back if I could only find that nippy

137

girl again, my heart's appointment, Mona Vera, and an ill wind blew no poppy good back where I started out, sadly and gaily enough, hoping for the best, knowing no better, or knowing no worse back there where she rolled over, disappeared, under it all, gone home, they told me, mother gone, to where she first was born, yes that was it, where she was born, they told me, a funny way to tell, and still not bad, a simple explanation, gone home awhelming, overwhelming, in that time, in that old house with the blue bed, a stone house, with pigeons up, under the eaves, the great trees swaying, great trees growing, great root growing, out of my bivalve heart, my pumpy place, involuntary muscle, come out of a door in her, a door with its muscle, the door in her, a bivalve vulva, where I went in, where I came out, and would go in again, gaily and sadly enough, back to buried life, find my whelming where it was, tell her I already paid, to enter, a womb of a whale aweigh in that strange Channel, this foggy place where all's soup, deserted and divided sea, and not a soul to be seen. Not a soul, anywhere. They call them souls.

Yet there's a soul right now, a lost soul. That crone again, old Coquelicots, old peekaboo, and I see you, for I'm still lost in circles. Lend me your compass, Coquelicots, drink and drown, take care of all swimming beasts. Lend me your compass, that's it. Lent. Bong, bong, yes, there's a bell, a slow bell, a low bell, a knell almost, almost a knell. It wends away, where I won't go. Yet would, almost. Sometime. Just to see. To see what really cooks upon that gothic stove. Sometime, some other time, some later time, not now. Love plays the deepsea catch, it's love will draw it in, so tack about, and there's the bone to cling to, the fished-up heart not changed as yet, and I'll turn home, I'll go home slowly now, if I could find that bridge again that I came over. I see a tree instead, a crosstree. No, it's moving, it's not a tree, it's a man, with his arms spread, directing traffic, in the fog. As if cars still existed. There's still lights. Streetlights. They've turned them on again, so people won't run into each other. They wouldn't want people to run into each other, make any contact, get tangled up in each other. No, it's not a traffic cop, it's a man feeding pigeons, some sort of guardian of the Cathedral, a watch-man, night-watchman, ready to turn in, his last act to feed the Dame's blear birds. He's got grain in his hands, his arms extended, the pigeons whirring, beating about his head, disappearing up, under the eaves, in the dark place, sooty place. I must be very close to Him, and he doesn't see me, sees only the birds. Maybe not so close. Distances are deceiving in a fog, ask any mariner. I'd ask him if he sees me, only he's gone, in a swirl. Ah, there's a hole again, no light in it, just a dead hole, like the eye of a hurricane. I'm in the still center, and two stories going on in my film at once, and someone's just adjusted the focus, so that there's her image clear in that little strip of film where wind has blown a hole, a niche up there, a statue in it, and two stories going on in my head at once with the candles guttering and that bird upon his pedestal turned round and they had rolled his life into a cave and put a stone in front and she said o god

139

the men that pass through this room yes the men that
have passed through this room I could tell you a story
or two about this hotel she said looking away and she
was something come to plague to destroy and here's a
statue whole again I see a mountain made of Saint-
Thérèse a word of shredded glass to look through there
in that high niche a Queen Mirror hung upon a rock
cathedral pealing bells of rock with upward thrusting
gothic branches in a shredded cloud there where the air
is shaken with light but there's too many stories to climb
and one of them going up and one of them down in my
head and she's gone to her long home when the sun
rolled round and klang klang bounced over buildings
into a pawnshop window where it hung with two other
balls that rang and the rooks called up under the eaves
and was I all those boys I used to be back then when I
climbed over wooden chairs when she came home with
her brassiere backwards in the dark dawn one time when
two songs already ran inside the dark of that film that
flowed across my eyes and a story in Ecclesiastes somewhere that summed it all up with a klang klang where
went my trolley down and off the line and that's the bell
for Sexolet's that rings me off at Aix-les-pains and hands
me down a book to find her in and she had only to be
awakened I had only to bring to her lips I had only to
see where the air is shaken with light in parables of sun
in fabulous fields of morning where she would say don't
stop oh god don't stop in the still time the rill time the
hill time when I came over her in the deep grass by the
Roman tracks where the wind blew and I had come and

140

I have come and I have come almost to the end of that indescribable journey almost into that far place where the blown music hung there where the statues have the look of loving to see a sudden leap of gothic as my umbered face would strike against that arched doortree and burst into that Virgin's place.

Save for the fact that all is keyless now and locked in old relentless Lent and if the stone-winged griffon fall my gargoyle waterspout is all I have to pour with here to cause her finally to open up, yes up, a scaffold here, some kind of scaffold for repairs, a spar upon a ship to climb and build my ship of death or life above the pews of oarsmen's seats above that bridge of altar with its chaliced compass set and groin of light above the pitching hold high up in that stone house in my boy's dream of flesh and ghost I'd find again up where the first birds were and curlews cawed and called, I see they've put her statues back together now up there as if to make Her whole again, I feel my funny phony face is on so square at last, my squarer self come back to find me where in a windless morning an endless time is blowing over foot-holding hills beyond a tolling town where she with longing hair comes swimming toward me with my hope and youth in a heavenhold of interpetaled love in a secret place in an acre of spring in the sweet grass at the end of the enchanted eleventh valley in the final fire where burns the world and I go kissing crowds to discover my Sunday wife.

But not so easy not so easy as all that to find sweet
purity on a stick old eskimo-pie-in-the-sky the greek chick
romanized and hung up in a niche comes out as something else again a crone again and coquelicots a cricket's
widow in a birchbark hat so found again fished up where
I still swim with one eye posted to each side like a fish
with a blind spot in front of the bow of the boat of flesh
an eye on each side like the player king on a playing card
a fishing king chief fishy one and in the country of the
blind the one-eyed man is king a sticky-wicket type he
is to push himself upon her with his biggest tool to liber-
ate her flesh as if he could and klang klang we're off
again on the ovarian trolley which has no place to go as
if there were no place to go besides heaven and hell if
that's to be imagined if anyone can possibly imagine
that because there must be someplace to go but heaven
and hell with my root still in earth still fixed in earth
still stuck in it as earth goes round with everybody upsidedown half of the time stuck feet-first into the earth
and sticking out from the earth in all directions like fil-
ings on a magnet each a little upsidedown pendulum
body swinging slightly each a little walking watch a
clock waving its arms in the sky and still a little time for
counting the saucers for the love in the closet will keep
the clothes will fit another student and I'll come back to
her to churchly her another time I'll come back to here
another time some other day when I'm feeling better
when I'm really ready for I'm not ready at all I'm not
ready yet for this strange scene for I'm still young and
it's not as if I were sixty-five looking around and asking
142

Where is everybody my god Just where in hell is everybody whom I started out with and that crowd of kids I ran around the corner with on Clancy Street up behind the waterworks Little Izzie with his snotrag and that Tom who pulled his pecker out to show us where the horse had bit behind the Ice Company sign and the firemen with their hoses out on the subway corner where I saw a girl with dirndl hoop and her communion dress all white when we ran round the corner with our baseball hats to play the Parkway Road Pirates and all of them still alive someplace now but still all pushed into the crypts of time to sleep so soundly with the dead that one same shadow blankets both confusing both and no way now to tell which one is still awake and I would like to think just like a Polly said that our history were noble and tragic and that our destiny were the same although I am myself a syndrome of a sin a flesh inferno daddy Dante never got to see as I go burning with my iron oxidizing in the air and who said *sssst* back then and crooked a finger at me beckoning to say O I want you but not like Uncle Sam in his disarmed forces poster no it's someone something else is calling I want you and I am coming yes I'm coming now yes wait I'm climbing finding falling trying to unhitch my parachute I hear a *hssst* I see someone up there in garbled goofy gargoyle place but I'll never make it I'll never make that scene like a Hogg among sinners a justified *cochon* even if I'm brave as nightbird now to bark like a bird in a bell and there's a knocking a knocking within or without a heart knocking or ringing or barking or looking within or with-

143

out a kind of discant a song backwards a low shout within me a plain chant a chain chant a grain of a groan by a holy groaner come after me a holy holler a wail of a note a death note with a voice in it to catch me as if I were already falling already dying although it occurs to me I'm still alive or still dead for the voice calls *Death Death* in a hermetic tension of an agony as if it were not dingy death itself but merely a full description of an hour of dying read aloud from a new newspaper printed white on black paper cut from larger reams of blackest toiletpaper printed with a death of light of life a light sprung up from earth in a passionate ascension of a voice beyond the world and I no more than a barrel rolling or a wheel cycling backwards through a time-bank or a time-ship whose high catwalk I'm walking across for I'm my own autodidact fallen off my cycle and always about to remount and my voice losing its leaves for I'm no longer anybody's son for I grew up against grownups and now myself am one against myself and yet have a long way to go and yet have only begun and I'll not float away quite yet in faery space my head in toiletpaper clouds unrolling I'll still stick around awhile and count the saucers so to see what comes, as if anything'd change, as if something else might develop, as if some other way might develop, as if some other alternative might show up, some other route from here through the foggy dew, through the eye of this needle, some other way out but up, some other route.

And I'll yet find a way I'll wenda-way out of this impasse where I mistook a solitude for

144

peace, but every way *out* turns out to be just another way *in*, another entrance, through which I can go back only into myself, in this no-mind noman's land my inter-zone, and there must be some other way of looking, some other way of seeing, out where most alone is most with self, in escape-city, in end-city where all climb out at end of line between a midnight and a bombnite at the end of the picture and the hero asleep in the soft arms, I'd sleep like that between nowhere and nowhere beat-ing about, I'm tired from seeing, and I'd go home so slowly now if I could find that crone again, my coqueli-cot, I'd cling to her, call her sweety, I'm your loverboy come home, your old al fresco lover come again, for I've got eyes for you in the flowered cages, and you could turn me on again, turn loose, I'd speak wild songs, say anything, I will I could I would, with an old bitch with gone teeth who'd still contain the ages, tenting tonight on the old campground, I'll rook you in your rucksack deary, and not a trick untried and not a train untaken not a tramway left to clank away to ends I never tried to see, for I've still tickets, I've still valid sticky tickets in my sticky hand to ride some other way around or through, there must be still some other way around eter-nity besides this stony ship with corkscrew stair up which I revolve more and more rapidly in a smaller and smaller space, in the smaller and smaller site of myself, like climbing up inside a pyramid or sliding down into a neck of hourglass in some crazy automat of a pinball city where punch a nickel and out you come, your sandy self comes draining through the final hole, and do they not

145

call that dying, what with every graveyard an automat
with its description of what's inside and the glass houses
with their little windows and Père Lachaise's creamy
crematorium with its smell of burnt toast and a new-
made widow watching through a little plate-glass window and then the tongueless ashes of some old blather-
skite with his big yack shut at last coming out in a little
hourglass replica of his body containing his sands and
all you have to do is turn him over and he'll begin again
his tickless way and the last time he saw Paris come back
again when he wore a bowler and striped pants and stood
on a café table singing the Marseillaise or some other
cornball ditty and bowing to the ladies before they carried him off on his sandy way where all runs down under
the hill in a pouring corner where all is laid with white
pieces of string and all made into ropes to climb up in
Our Dame's café without no pants to tear upon the nails
to hook him up upon a cross a fish without no hands or
fins but a tail of sound and fury signifying no one but
my fuzzy fungus self old fuckywuzzy fish inside a loaf
of brain still hungry to be friggin youse up your anni-
versary of paddybuns and a bird in hand that maketh
two in a bush whenever possible before the slippy cock
cries out his last so roll me over once again my mother's
one my two-to-one my tilley-valley lady sex-haiku upon
a stem old passionflower blooming yearly buxom baby
annalivie brassy lassy I'll yet hold you dearly treat you
cavalierly in your five-and-ten brassiere old holy grail
old golden fleece and golden snatch and pussy with a
Giaconda smile and all the girls Jerusalem threw out my
146

Milly Bloom my Lola Lola sweater-girl with Coca-Cola a swingy chick a sweetie-pie a swell girl a goose girl a goosy girl a sweet bitch a rich dish a prickly miss a true tin angel on a stick a Lady Loverly a nice Miss Douce a happy hag upon the loose a matelot's mistress a sailor's sistress a lover's pie a pie-bed a mat of flesh a bed of down where I'd bed down and roll you over once again with your corona round your head and who's the one that fitted you with that when all should know to deify is to betray in a failure of love in some sort of transaction with myself.

And all those women's shadows caught on a tree and stretched like a rubberband or a piece of string and all become one shadow of she who is not the subject of my story for I myself am the subject of my sentence and she's the object and I've diagrammed it all and analyzed the syntax of my sentence in which she's the object and it's an objective case and she is her in this case which is the case of myself before the court yes the case of a mad cyclist in the sky disturbing the peace and a priest with his sky-hook reaching out to catch me in a falling away through a failure of contact through a failure of life in an air of despair in face of the final insoluble problem the whole human perplexity of the final vernal annihilation where lucidity is reserved for those who do not love where if to deify is to betray Our Dame will drown in her own halo for it's no life-ring to be buoyed on and I still trying to unhitch my parachute so aura me not and ora me no pro nobis for I'll be off on my own I'll fly away I'll drop away and my paper photo blown upon the street with the story of my syntax writ down in obit like as if I was certain to die a certain falling way when my pinball machine registers tilt and the who and the why of it still unclear when all discovered so far is that consciousness itself is the only tangible happiness and me a real mixed-up cat as anybody trailing me around and up in this fog would be sure to see if love made them lucid enough to see anything in this site of myself made into the reassuring form of a story in which I see myself the gay and lucid one hanging from a high hook between a being and a nothingness upon a coming Quasimodo Sunday to be my own voyeur until I die with a big sound a low sound and a big thud and so become again a nouveau-né a neophite upon a breast and quasi modo géniti indeed and God not a her and God not a he but an It and this It the power by which the eye hears and the ear speaks in no popish purple paradise of gysmjoy fallen down upon the pigeon's grass nor at any tropic where a vulva blooms and grows in the blowing weather of a heaven of fair flesh fields where God is something or other where God is something we have in common and heaven no rest home among the galaxies. Though I still climb up to finger those chimeras with the original little black book of life in my hand a misguided missal telling over the catechism of my life in the tall tale of a dropsical death by a dropsical kid or a cat and I'll die the death of what I am already and not what I might have been trying to get out of my skin and thus skinning myself down to *nada* and finally jumping up in some Easter pulpit shouting God is dead in a dark night a blear night of dear sense where every ascent requires an assent for I'm still on the surface of things still wanting to paint my mountains of hungry flesh my brush a horn of plenty my horn a longfellow myself an unfunny falstaff of a hill of flesh a gargantua of paint a walking sack of salt made into a friday fish to hang upon the old hook a Leonardo of the absurd with his angel of annunciation and much too fat to climb to any holy heights.

But I'm still not ready to hang on my hook I still got things to straighten out still got a lot of earlier scenes to go over I've still got thoughts to think and even at my tender age I got memories to mull over and call my own like when I was first free and easy and sprung out hungry on the world and spilled my seed for the first holy time that year wandering about in various fertile fields up and down the land like a dinosaur goofing about the land-scape and quite precocious at that I'll admit when I called her and she had a red capote I mean I'll turn the tail around I mean she had a capochino a capodistra down on the Riviera and three or two times my age and when I called her on the phone that time she said right off God will you love me I want to love you I feel a void I want to feel you in me filling me But when I got up there to her cool villa all she wanted to do was talk with words and she told me The Nazz will get you in the end yes that's what she told me I remember now The Nazz will get you in the end as if some kind of snowman come down from the hills with a cross for a cane would hook

and snow me like that old guy with a cross-stick used to
be hired to spear papers in a village square and I used
to talk to him walking around because he was like some
kind of traveler from a far place and had a pet raccoon
he used to let me feed walking around the park and him
looking like Christ with his beard and his sandals saying
a hail mary mother of grace as he went with his pet raccoon on a string and his big cross of a stick but then that
year lost his picking job and got run out of town all at
once because he didn't like the government and when
the war in Indo-China was coming and they were send-
ing the soldiers he climbed up on the town church steeple and wouldn't come down like some Saint Stylites as
if he could stop the war single-handed by not coming
down until they stopped but one dark night they got
him down and carried him off kicking and yelling like
the original beat Christ with his beat haircut and sandals
and beat beard and everybody agreeing he was crazy
the way he carried on about what's holding Heaven up
in the sky and how people shouldn't waste it on the sky
and how someday it would fall down on top of everybody anyway because there must be gravity in heaven
too and everything that went up must come down and
anyway that was the last I saw of him, and I see now,
I am just beginning to see, how all these stray things add
up and everybody adds up to the same thing and the
damn thing's still growing and this movie made-up out
of a lot of parts of other people's films all glued together
and one life is a lot of people's lives hung together in
space only it's all kept in the dark it's all kept coiled away
150

except for one small frame at a time flashed upon the screen of the present and out I come and out everybody comes from their cradles carelessly rocking and the various women I've known all adding up to flash in a composite image all leading up to this moment in some lost connection with this Virgin's place, and there I come and there I came with that first one back then I used to call on the phone who didn't see any difference between Christ and Buddha and she'd just Christianize Buddha a little and he'd never notice just sitting there in his full lotus position with the incense coming out of the holes in his head and in fact he'd have nothing at all against a little private conversation with Christ although they'd probably have a lot of differences which maybe should be settled in advance by undersecretaries of state before they agreed to meet at the summit on TV not to mention all the language barriers and so forth yes and she used to talk all the time about how Buddha would really dig having a personal interview with Christ's God although he wasn't much on chatting in Latin and it would all have to be done without words and in fact there wouldn't be any words to get in the way between them and then heaven might really fall down on the whole scene and the world's crisis would be over forever like if it was really semantics that made wars well then wow turn off all words and look in each other's eyes and be like birds, and she used to rave on like that but she no Zen-freak in a Sits-bath when I called that time she kept telling me over the phone how she lived only to come and would I come with her each time she came and would I come as long as she did every time and so on all about how she knew there would be a second coming and the telephone a marvelous instrument for all that and she probably with the end of it in her mouth or some other place as she was talking it got so hot and the telephone company reporting a hot line a red button flashing somewhere on a switchboard and there's a passage in Episcopalians to explain all that but who stole cock's robin and who stole robin's cock back then when I couldn't make it couldn't make the scene with her and then where gone the fancy airs she had where gone her hipness and her sexy voice when she lay down where none would lay with her except Bad Deeds and hair of grass blow over her in the public domain in a nowhere time which is the place I'm going and the place I've already been for I'm strictly from noplace now and yet still going there where soon is late and tell me tell me what's myself except a holy site that's been vacated and still to be returned to in the still center the eye of the storm the still mad center of the *sturm und drang* and here we are again and there I am again and there you am again and there she am again and there her am again and again growing out of a pot by the far side of a far shore in the Queen's Road at nightfall and never a gayer one to say you true sweet picklepuss sweet everyman to lie with you without good deeds.

And so through Beckett's wicket and the American woods in the long return with old eternal Her o lady in a cran of light with hidden breasts I hang to hold and everything now reduced to

152

a history of climbing and falling although I'm not my pouring concrete father on his skyscraping scaffolding falling spreadeagled into a vat of Christus Cement and the history of falling the history of looking for love in a high place and all life seen as a series of orgasms in a sequence of other acts in a vaster way of seeing particular things in a hungry turning of a plaster head on a night journey through a lost place in a far field where I took off her clothes for the first time and felt her heart that pounded underneath like a buried little train so dark upon its tracks and shaking flesh of earth.

But light is in my eyes up here, it's growing stronger all the time, there where the air is shaken with light, and I'll grow yet to my long home where I'm the noise at the threshold of voiceless silence, where only the fourth person singular remains, the voice of the bee is all that remains and it's the vacated soul of myself and five flights up yes it seems I've always lived five flights up and here I am again on a tower with the sun at the top in a smaller and smaller space although I've forgotten the number of the house and I was right about the street but wrong about the house and I am right about this street but wrong about this house for the Ideal still lives on the Other Side of the Street and it's maybe her sister I want, and her blue breasts are over my shoulder and her blue breasts become the sky, but where does the round moon live, and where do the models keep their clothes, for I still have eyes for them, although one of my eyes must have been sold by now, leaving me but one movable eye

153

on one side of a fishhead, or on one side of a sleeper
between dreams upon a hook of a last wall of childhood,
and my organ turned into a golem voice beyond the
world that will not weep among the dark pines and shattered shadows among the last of children where my
saltpeter melts away and dreams continue in other
dreams, and which city is it with such strange street
signs way down below all pointing nowhere except up
here where the road ends in air where one *escollier* disappeared in history yet left a turtle's voice behind, and
all that's left is that long thirst of self a blind man has
to see his own desilvered face, and my eye blinks when
the scene shifts, and this all took place between two
blinks in a confusing of sex with love where I would be
a bird to fall without a wing, but where do the birds go
when they die if they already are men's souls, and I say
up, I answer up, as if their pigeon wings could evade
every assent still being a descent of mind, a falling away
of intellect, as if to say Well I give up, I finally admit
that man is made for prayers sweet melodies and aspiration, and it's all in her in her cool niche right here, as if
she couldn't exist except in this stone house and never
really did or could fall through or out of her stained glass
window into the bright adventure of the street, and like
man don't hand me all that jass, for I didn't want to fall
up here anyway, and we're so brave and blowing scorn
out of our horn when we're all well and wailing like a
young dog barking at a bear behind a safety fence, but
then when the fury falls then who's the first to run away
telltale between his legs and who's the first to grovel dad
154

to pray hail mary mother I want you I see a mountain made of Saint Thérèse, not sexual and not symbolic but the thing itself upon a stick, and falling down in adoration and pure fear the wigged one says just like a saint Don't hang me up on rationality or any kind of reasonscene because you can't prove anything with words and like the Daddy-priest says you can't prove the existence of God except by faith, which all requires a teleological suspension of ethics, no matter what you jazzcat-jesuits and breadwine missionaries say to the contrary about making the two scenes at once. And lo old mama earth Miss Gravity still exercise her fatal attraction, as our falling is what falling does and who's to know when I wing down into the public domain just what Somebody could have meant by me and what could He possibly have had in mind, as if I were really seriously supposed to be a reflexive pronoun reflecting parastatic Him, but what the cricket says and does are two different things, and wiggy fat upon the bone will fall as fast as he who's thin, as he who's been where I halfhope to go without a formal passing through a Dark Night of the official stony route through dispossession of myself into some other All outside myself, as if I might still make it off into the true blue with a gloss and a glib or a simple I love you buddha-baby you're so cool to me and kool tastes so good like a buddha should, and there's a tale in Krishnamurti to explain all that, as if amok in Mexico all I had to do was dig and kiss the tinfoil tits of Guadalupe and so take a fix at any old altar where the Nazz is still hung-up waiting for me after straightening the cat

155

with the bent frame, as here I come climbing still to cast myself upon the lillypads, thinking crooked to see straight, old brainstorm me with genius-mind at work above beyond behind the scenes and behind the scene of myself, paring my nails and refining them and myself as well out of existence in a suspension of disbelief to persuade myself that bread is really god's own loot, and so end up my own dumb Juggler of Our Dame so pure and true to innocence of words I'd juggle to unhang myself before the king and queen and map my own apocalypse in a panic of idols conning the world, my mirror losing its desilvered sight, and all our dames telescoped together in a film too black and white with its figures only paper in a here and now that are no more and no more me, my teeth are floats and I cry goon to stop and look and listen now no more a trilogy of twine around the genitals in visions made of pot that make me think that I can fly or be any miscellaneous man falling away waving genitals and manuscripts to come at last to see to conquer nada with a string tied round to see no hear no know no evil in a total world of con to flip my lovely over with a hail to naked mary as I come, although I still would go away, I still would break away, I still might turn away, if I could get away somewhere I'd be a buddhist in a cave to paint a different kind of holy on a wall somewhere or make a different kind of statue on some temple lost in Konarak, were I not tangled up and trussed in all these ropes of string I stole, and still come back to make my own stone angel in the living end o dark of hair I'm climbing up between her knockers now I see

156

the grass of falling hair nailed up in pigeon caw the moondial clocks to stop with string and our loose ends the ones that hang us after all and me with nothing here to prove I'm even a member of the club although I've got a member almost identical to everyone's member and no hood on it though I started out gaily and sadly enough and hid in it and rose again on the seventh day and came forth finally in this hung place where there's some clapper broken loose that clouts away the final fog and swings and sings upon the wind I break, the wind I break to climb.

And so see now my blown newspaper once again tossed up upon that wind with my obituary writ in it ahead of time so all I have to do is give them a head for it even if a letter's printed backward in one line and all I have to do is give them my head and I'm off to see the wizard the wonderful wizard of odds against me in the nowhere void and nothing more to kiss and no more eyes and longing hair as when that time under the great trees where the crickets were, suddenly she stopt laughing, put my hands upon her breasts, and then, and so, and then so down and down we go, my granite dangle hanging down to dive through flesh of air, I smear my forehead ash my white skin sandals on I see dawn's angels stoned for good I see green lights turn yellow in the mad brain dust the tar roofs bleed I see God grips the genitals to catch illusionary me stunned down in air of death's insanity to kiss me off he plays the deepsea catch he reels me in O god

LAWRENCE FERLINGHETTI was born in Yonkers, New York in 1919. He received an A.B. degree from the University of North Carolina and an M.A. from Columbia University. After Navy service in World War II, he "emptied wastebaskets at *Time*" for a while and then lived in Paris (1947–51) where he received a Doctorat de l'Université from the Sorbonne. On his return he went to San Francisco where he and Peter D. Martin founded the first all-paperbound bookstore in the U.S., City Lights. Under its imprint, Ferlinghetti began publishing the Pocket Poets Series which includes work by William Carlos Williams, Allen Ginsberg, Kenneth Patchen, Kenneth Rexroth, Denise Levertov, Gregory Corso, as well as Ferlinghetti's own collection of poems, *Pictures of the Gone World*. He is the author of a second book of poetry, *A Coney Island of the Mind,* published in 1958 by New Directions. His first novel *Her* was published in 1960. *Starting From San Francisco*, new poems, with a 7 inch LP Record of the poet reading selections from the book, was published in 1961. Ferlinghetti has travelled widely in this country giving poetry readings, and in 1960 he participated with Allen Ginsberg in a Pan-American cultural conference at the University of Concepción in Chile. His *Tentative Description of a Dinner Given to Promote the Impeachment of President Eisenhower and Other Poems* and *Poetry Readings in the Cellar* are on Fantasy LP recordings (#7002 and #7004).

NEW DIRECTIONS PAPERBOOKS

Send for free catalogue describing all Paperbooks
NEW DIRECTIONS   333 Sixth Avenue   New York 14